THE DILLON PRESS
CHILDREN'S
ATLAS

THE DILLON PRESS
CHILDREN'S
ATLAS

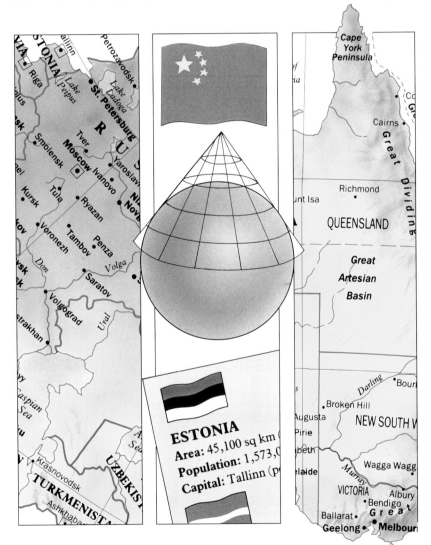

MALCOLM PORTER

DILLON PRESS
New York

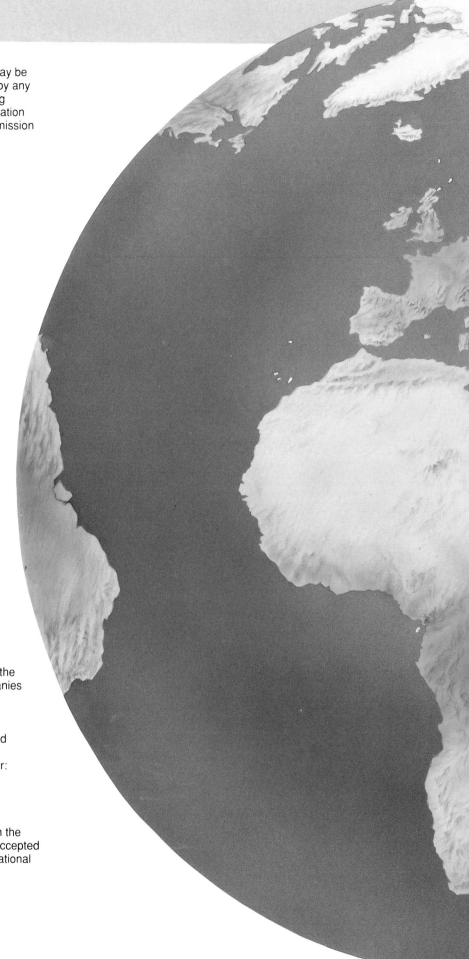

A Cherrytree Book

Designed and produced by
A S Publishing
Consultant editor Keith Lye
Assistant editor Paul Dempsey

First published 1993
by Cherrytree Press Limited

First American publication 1993
by Dillon Press, Macmillan Publishing Company, 866 Third Avenue, New York, NY 10022

Macmillan Publishing Company is part of the Maxwell Communication Group of Companies

10 9 8 7 6 5 4 3 2 1

Printed in Hong Kong by Colorcraft Limited

Library of Congress Catalog Card Number:
93 - 15593
ISBN 0 - 87518 - 606 - 8

The statistics used in this atlas come from the United Nations and other internationally accepted sources, together with recent data from national censuses when available.

CONTENTS

Planet Earth

Our earth is one of the nine planets that circle the sun. It is the third planet from the sun. Today we can see photographs of the earth taken from space. These show land areas, called continents, and blue seas and oceans.

Maps show the same things, but they give much more information than space photographs. They show the names and positions of cities and towns and other features, such as rivers and mountains.

Sun

Mercury
Venus
Earth
Mars
Jupiter
Saturn
Uranus
Neptune
Pluto

As the earth circles the sun, it spins on its axis, an imaginary line joining the North Pole, the center of the earth, and the South Pole.

Some lines appear on maps. One line around the middle of the earth, exactly halfway between the North and South poles, is called the equator. Other lines are called the Tropic of Cancer in the northern half of the world and the Tropic of Capricorn in the southern half. Two important lines go around the cold areas near the poles. They are the Arctic and Antarctic circles.

North Pole

Arctic Circle
Axis
Tropic of Cancer
Equator
Tropic of Capricorn
Antarctic Circle

South Pole

Continents			
Continent	Area (sq miles)	Area (sq km)	Population
North America	9,363,000	24,249,000	419,000,000
South America	6,886,000	17,835,000	298,000,000
Europe	4,066,000	10,532,000	698,000,000
Asia	16,968,000	43,947,000	3,202,000,000
Africa	11,694,000	30,330,000	669,000,000
Australia	2,968,000	7,687,000	17,073,000
Antarctica	5,400,000	14,000,000	None permanent

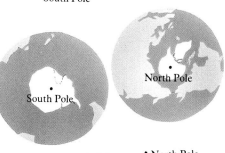

South Pole

North Pole

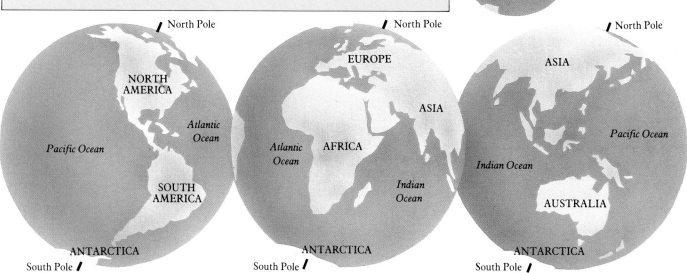

North Pole

NORTH AMERICA

Atlantic Ocean

Pacific Ocean

SOUTH AMERICA

ANTARCTICA

South Pole

North Pole

EUROPE

ASIA

Atlantic Ocean

AFRICA

Indian Ocean

ANTARCTICA

South Pole

North Pole

ASIA

Pacific Ocean

Indian Ocean

AUSTRALIA

ANTARCTICA

South Pole

World records

Mountains
The highest mountains in five continents are shown on the right. The world's highest peak is Mount Everest.

Everest (ASIA) 29,028ft (8,848m)

Aconcagua (SOUTH AMERICA) 22,831ft (6,959m)

McKinley (NORTH AMERICA) 20,320ft (6,194m)

Kilimanjaro (AFRICA) 19,340ft (5,895m)

Elbrus (EUROPE) 18,481ft (5,633m)

Rivers
The world's longest rivers are the Nile in Africa and the Amazon in South America.

Darling (AUSTRALIA) 1,702 miles (2,739 km)

Volga (EUROPE) 2,194 miles (3,531 km)

Mississippi (NORTH AMERICA) 2,348 miles (3,779 km)

Chang Jiang (ASIA) 3,436 miles (5,530 km)

Amazon (SOUTH AMERICA) 4,007 miles (6,448 km)

Nile (AFRICA) 4,145 miles (6,670 km)

Deserts
Deserts cover about one seventh of the world's land areas. The Sahara in North Africa is the largest.

Sahara (AFRICA) 3,250,000 sq miles (8,400,000 sq km)

Great Australian Desert (AUSTRALIA) 600,000 sq miles (1,550,000 sq km)

Arabian Desert (ASIA) 500,000 sq miles (1,300,000 sq km)

Gobi Desert (ASIA) 450,000 sq miles (1,170,000 sq km)

Kalahari Desert (AFRICA) 200,000 sq miles (520,000 sq km)

Lakes
The world's largest lake is the Caspian Sea, so called because its water is salty. The largest freshwater lake is Lake Superior.

Lake Superior (NORTH AMERICA) 31,700 sq miles (82,100 sq km)

Lake Huron (NORTH AMERICA) 23,000 sq miles (59,570 sq km)

Aral Sea (ASIA) 15,600 sq miles (40,400 sq km)

Caspian Sea (ASIA/EUROPE) 143,000 sq miles (371,000 sq km)

Lake Michigan (NORTH AMERICA) 22,300 sq miles (57,750 sq km)

Lake Victoria (AFRICA) 26,828 sq miles (69,500 sq km)

Islands
Islands are land areas surrounded by water. The world's largest island, Greenland, is mostly covered by ice.

New Guinea (OCEANIA) 300,000 sq miles (792,500 sq km)

Baffin Island (NORTH AMERICA) 195,928 sq miles (507,528 sq km)

Greenland (NORTH AMERICA) 840,000 sq miles (2,175,000 sq km)

Borneo (ASIA) 280,000 sq miles (725,450 sq km)

Madagascar (AFRICA) 226,658 sq miles (587,040 sq km)

Deeps and depressions
The deepest point on land is the shore of the Dead Sea in Israel and Jordan. The deepest part of the oceans is in the Marianas Trench, in the Pacific.

Lowest point on land
Dead Sea shoreline (ASIA) 1,312ft (400m) below sea level

Deepest point in the Oceans
Marianas Trench (PACIFIC OCEAN) 36,198ft (11,034m)

Deepest Lake
Lake Baykal (ASIA) 6,365ft (1,940m) deep or 4,872ft (1,485m) below sea level

7

Measuring the Earth

Models of the earth are called globes. The surfaces of globes are marked with networks of lines.

Some lines run around the globe. They are called lines of latitude, or parallels. The equator, the tropics of Cancer and Capricorn, and the Arctic and Antarctic circles are all lines of latitude.

Other lines on globes run at right angles to the lines of latitude, through both the North and South poles. These are lines of longitude, or meridians.

Lines of latitude and longitude are marked on maps, which show the globe, or parts of it, on flat pieces of paper. The position of every place on earth has its own latitude and longitude.

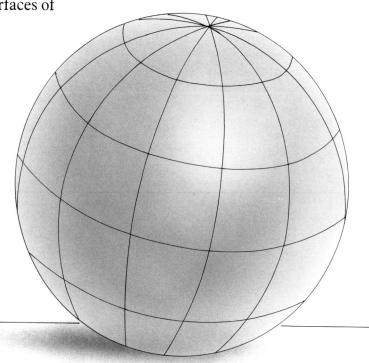

Latitude

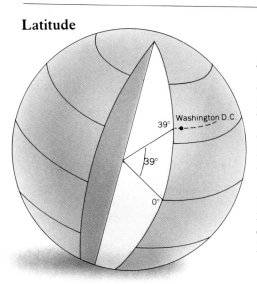

The latitude of the equator, which divides the earth into two equal halves, called hemispheres, is 0°. The latitude of the North Pole is 90 degrees north (90°N), while the latitude of the South Pole is 90 degrees south (90°S).

The latitude of places between the equator and the poles is measured in degrees north or south of the equator. For example, the latitude of Washington, D.C. is nearly 39 degrees north. This means that the angle formed at the center of the earth between the equator and Washington, D.C. is nearly 39 degrees.

The Tropic of Cancer is latitude 23½ degrees north, while the Tropic of Capricorn is 23½ degrees south. The Arctic Circle is 66½ degrees north, while the Antarctic Circle is 66½ degrees south.

Longitude

Lines of longitude are measured 180° east and west of the prime meridian, or 0° longitude. The prime meridian runs through the North Pole, Greenwich in London, England, and the South Pole. The line was agreed to at an international conference in 1884.

Washington, D.C., for example, is situated 77° west. This means that the angle formed at the center of the earth between the prime meridian and another line of longitude running through Washington, D.C. is 77° west of the prime meridian.

The 180° line of longitude east and west of the prime meridian runs through the Pacific Ocean, on the far side of the world from the prime meridian. The prime meridian and the 180° line of longitude divide the earth into two hemispheres, east and west, in the same way that the equator divides north and south.

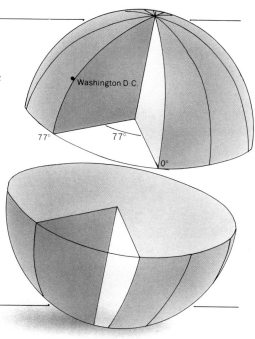

Map projections

One of the problems faced by map-makers is that it is impossible to show the earth on a flat piece of paper without distorting it to some extent. You can understand the problem if you imagine that the world is an orange. If you peel the orange, there is no way you can stretch the peel flat without breaking it up and crushing the pieces.

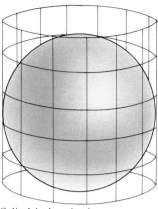

Azimuthal projection

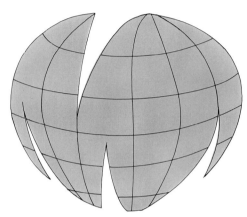

To solve this problem, map-makers use map projections.

Imagine a glass globe with the network of lines of latitude and longitude, or graticules, engraved on it. Put a light inside the globe and the graticules will be cast, or projected, onto a flat sheet of paper touching it at one point to produce an *azimuthal projection*. Imagine doing the same with a paper cylinder to produce a *cylindrical projection* or a paper cone to produce a *conical projection*.

Cylindrical projection

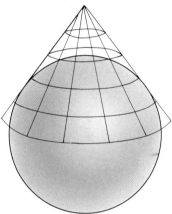

Conical projection

Projections in this atlas

The projections shown above are called perspective projections. But, in practice, map-makers seldom use these projections. Instead, they use projections that they develop using mathematics, so that they can accurately reproduce areas, shapes, distances, and directions. Projections used for maps of the world can preserve some of these features, though no single projection can show them all.

The maps that show the continent at the beginning of each chapter of this atlas have been specially drawn to show how the continent looks from space. The map on the right shows how Africa on page 69 would look with lines of latitude and longitude.

How to Use The Dillon Press Children's Atlas

To put as much information as possible on a map, map-makers use symbols. To get the most out of the maps in this atlas, it helps to know the symbols:

Cities with a population of more than 1 million people	**New York City** •
Cities with a population between 100,000 and 1 million	**Atlantic City** •
Towns with a population of below 100,000	Vineland •
Capital city	**Washington D.C.** ▣
State capital	★ **Phoenix**
Mountain with its height	△ *Mt. McKinley 20,320ft*
Mountain range	**Catskill Mts**
Dam	—┤—
Island	*Island*
Archaeological site	∴

River Canal Lake	*River* *Canal* *Lake*
Country name	**CANADA**
Province or state name	MARYLAND
Border	——————

Key to land coloring

Forest	
Crops	
Dry Grassland	
Desert	
Tundra	
Polar	

Maps in the atlas

The Dillon Press Children's Atlas starts with views of the world as a whole. The physical map of the world on pages 12-13 shows the world's main land features, while the political map on pages 14-15 shows the countries into which the world is divided.

The atlas contains sections on North America, South America, Europe, Asia, Africa, and Australia. Each section has a map showing where the continent is situated on the globe and the countries it contains. Other maps show groups of countries (or states) in the continent.

If you want to know facts about a country, such as its population or area, look at the table alongside the map.

The last section of the atlas has maps of the oceans and the polar regions.

Populations

Many large cities, such as Boston, have metropolitan area populations (2,871,000) that are greater than the city figures (574,000). Such cities have larger dot sizes on the map to emphasize their importance.

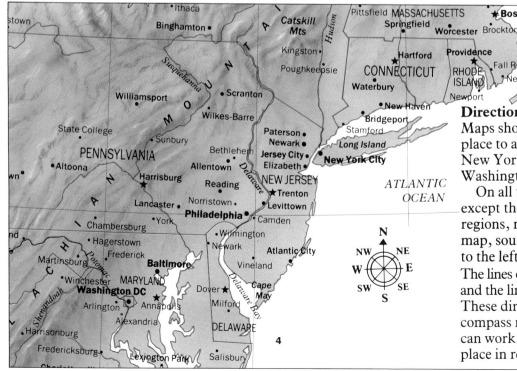

Direction finding

Maps show the direction from one place to another. For example, New York City lies northeast of Washington, D.C.

On all the maps in this atlas, except those showing the polar regions, north lies at the top of the map, south at the bottom, west lies to the left, and east is to the right. The lines of longitude go north-south and the lines of latitude go east-west. These directions are also shown on compass roses on each map, so you can work out the direction of one place in relation to another.

Using the index

To find a place in this atlas, use the index at the back of the book.

After each place name you will find a number and then a letter and a number. For example, if you want to find Rome, the capital of Italy, you will find the following entry in the index:

Rome **52** B3

You should then turn to page 52, where you will find the map of Italy and Southeastern Europe. Look for the square on the map labeled B at the top and 3 on the left-hand side. You will then find Rome in that square.

Scales and distance

Maps are drawn to scale. This means that you can find the distance between places on a map.

The maps in this atlas have a scale line marked in miles and kilometers. Place a piece of paper on this line and mark off the distances shown. If you want to know the distance from San Diego to Lake Havasu City, place your piece of paper on the map with the zero end on San Diego. You will find that the distance to Lake Havasu City is about 200 miles (300 kilometers). See if you can find the distance between Cedar City and Flagstaff.

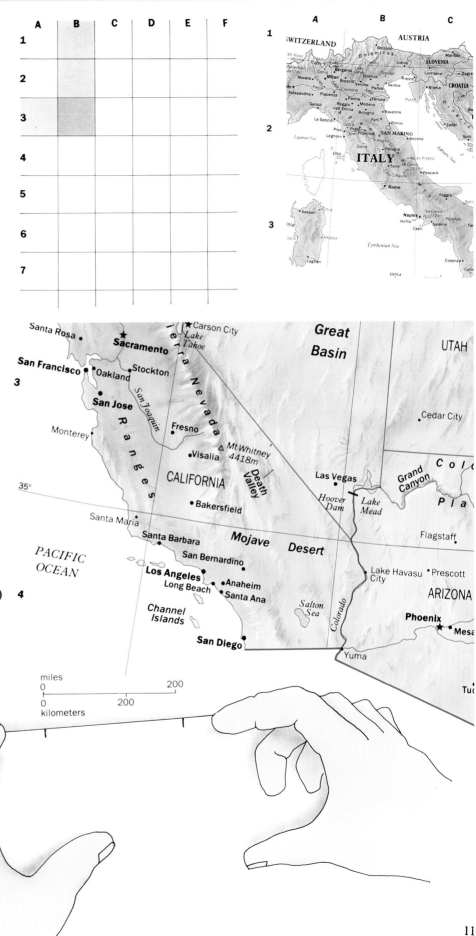

The Physical World

ARCTIC OCEAN

Baffin
Island

Greenland

Arctic Circle

Mt McKinley

R o c k y   M t s

Hudson
Bay

Great
Plains

Great Lakes

Appalachian Mts

**NORTH
AMERICA**

Mississippi

Tropic of Cancer

Gulf of
Mexico

West
Indies

ATLANTIC
OCEAN

Caribbean Sea

Equator

PACIFIC   OCEAN

A
n
d
e
s

Amazon

Selvas

Atacama Desert

M
t
s

**SOUTH
AMERICA**

Tropic of Capricorn

△ Aconcagua

Tasman
Sea

New
Zealand

Patagonia

Antarctic Circle

ANTARCTICA

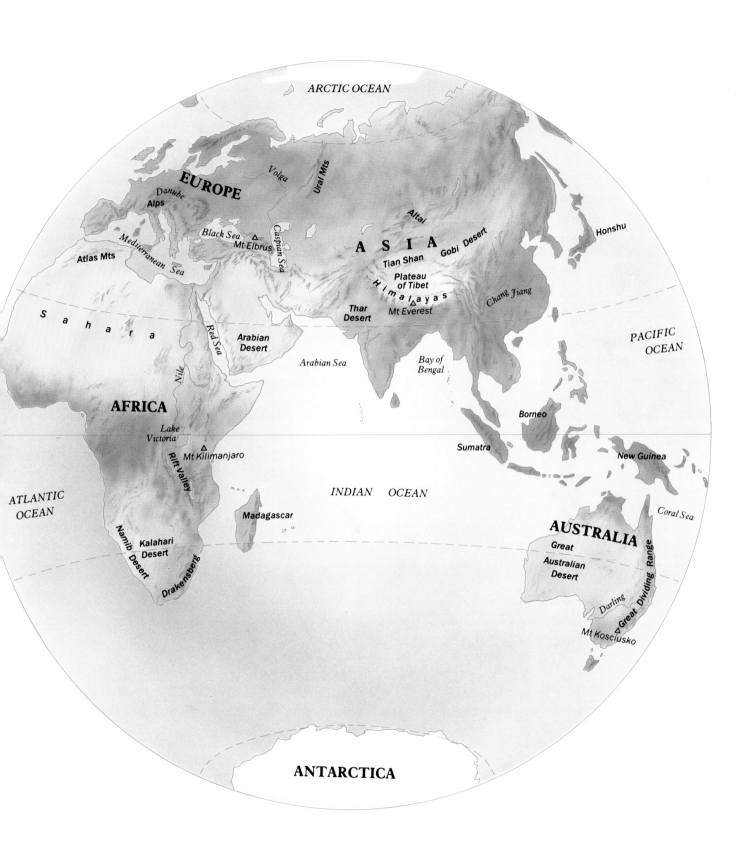

ARCTIC OCEAN

EUROPE

Volga

Ural Mts

Danube

Alps

Altai

ASIA

Black Sea

Mt Elbrus

Caspian Sea

Tian Shan

Gobi Desert

Honshu

Atlas Mts

Mediterranean Sea

Plateau
of Tibet

Chang Jiang

PACIFIC
OCEAN

H i m a l a y a s

S a h a r a

Red Sea

Thar
Desert

Mt Everest

Arabian
Desert

Nile

Arabian Sea

Bay of
Bengal

AFRICA

Borneo

Lake
Victoria

Sumatra

New Guinea

Mt Kilimanjaro

Rift Valley

INDIAN   OCEAN

ATLANTIC
OCEAN

Madagascar

AUSTRALIA

Coral Sea

Namib Desert

Kalahari
Desert

Great

Australian

Desert

Drakensberg

Darling

Great Dividing Range

Mt Kosciusko

ANTARCTICA

The Political World

The world is divided into more than 200 countries. The biggest country is the Russian Federation. The smallest independent country is Vatican City, which covers only 109 acres (44 hectares) in Rome, Italy's capital city.

Most of the world's countries are independent, but some are dependencies — that is, they are ruled by other countries. French Guiana on this map is not an independent country. It is ruled as an overseas region of France.

Most dependencies are tiny island countries. They are so small that they do not appear on this map. The map of the Caribbean on pages 32 and 33 shows several tiny dependencies not shown on this map. They include Montserrat (U.K.), Martinique (France), and the Netherlands Antilles.

AND

NORWAY
FINLAND
SWEDEN
UNITED KINGDOM
DENMARK
ESTONIA
LATVIA
LITHUANIA
RELAND
NETHERLANDS
BELGIUM
GERMANY
POLAND
BELARUS
LUXEMBOURG
CZECHOSLOVAKIA
UKRAINE
SWITZERLAND
AUSTRIA
HUNGARY
MOLDOVA
FRANCE
6
ROMANIA
1
2
4
5
9
7
8
BULGARIA
GEORGIA
RTUGAL
SPAIN
ITALY
10
TURKEY
ARMENIA
AZERBAIJAN
GREECE
CYPRUS
SYRIA
TURKMENISTAN
TAJIKISTAN
MALTA
TUNISIA
LEBANON
ISRAEL
IRAQ
IRAN
AFGHANISTAN
MOROCCO
JORDAN
KUWAIT
BAHRAIN
QATAR
U.A.E.
SAUDI ARABIA
OMAN
PAKISTAN
NEPAL
BHUTAN
RN SAHARA
ALGERIA
LIBYA
EGYPT
URITANIA
MALI
NIGER
CHAD
SUDAN
YEMEN
BANGLADESH
INDIA
MYANMAR
BURKINA FASO
DJIBOUTI
UINEA
EONE
GHANA
NIGERIA
CENTRAL AFRICAN REPUBLIC
ETHIOPIA
SOMALI REPUBLIC
THAILAND
VIETNAM
CAMBODIA
BERIA
COTE D'IVOIRE
CAMEROON
UGANDA
KENYA
SRI LANKA
MALAYSIA
SINGAPORE
BRUNEI
SAO TOME & PRINCIPE
GABON
CONGO
RWANDA
BURUNDI
EQUATORIAL GUINEA
ZAIRE
TANZANIA
COMOROS
ANGOLA
ZAMBIA
MALAWI
ZIMBABWE
MOZAMBIQUE
NAMIBIA
BOTSWANA
MADAGASCAR
SWAZILAND
SOUTH AFRICA
LESOTHO

RUSSIAN FEDERATION

KAZAKHSTAN
UZBEKISTAN
KYRGYZSTAN
MONGOLIA
NORTH KOREA
SOUTH KOREA
JAPAN
CHINA
TAIWAN
LAOS
PHILIPPINES
INDONESIA
PAPUA NEW GUINEA
SOLOMON ISLANDS

AUSTRALIA

NEW ZEALAND

1 ANDORRA
2 MONACO
3 LIECHTENSTEIN
4 SAN MARINO
5 VATICAN CITY
6 SLOVENIA
7 CROATIA
8 YUGOSLAVIA
9 BOSNIA & HERCEGOVINA
10 ALBANIA
11 MACEDONIA

Information panels

This atlas contains panels with information about all the independent countries of the world, including their area, population and capital. Extra details, including information about religions, languages, the economy or main products, and the nature of the government, are given about as many countries as space allows.

Many countries are republics, with a president as head of state. Most republics are democracies,

with elected parliaments, though some republics are not democratic.

Other countries are monarchies. Their head of state is a king or queen, though most are actually ruled by elected governments. Some major countries in the British Commonwealth, such as Australia, Canada, and New Zealand recognize the British queen as their head of state, but in practice democratically elected governments rule these countries.

North America

North America, the third largest continent, contains the world's largest island, Greenland, and three huge countries: Canada, the United States, and Mexico. It also includes the smaller countries of Central America and the islands of the Caribbean Sea.

The land of North America includes icy areas in the north and warm tropical places in the south. The United States contains both the Mississippi-Missouri River, North America's longest, and the highest mountain, Mount McKinley in Alaska.

North America contains 23 independent countries. Its total population is about 420 million. Canada and the United States are rich, developed countries. But many people of Central America and the Caribbean are poor.

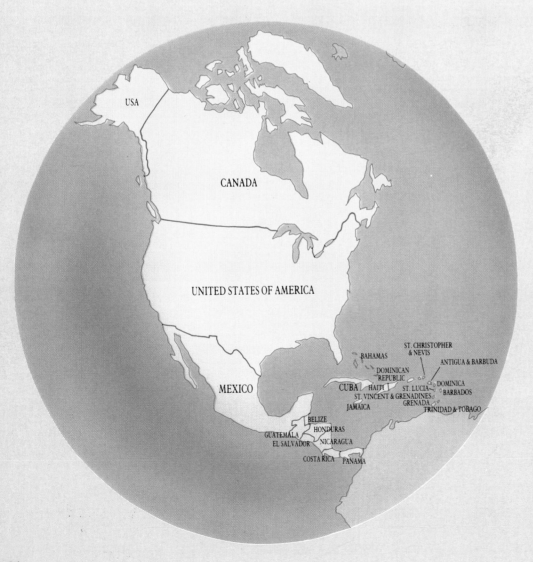

USA
CANADA
UNITED STATES OF AMERICA
MEXICO
BAHAMAS
ST. CHRISTOPHER & NEVIS
ANTIGUA & BARBUDA
DOMINICAN REPUBLIC
DOMINICA
CUBA
HAITI
ST. LUCIA
BARBADOS
ST. VINCENT & GRENADINES
GRENADA
JAMAICA
TRINIDAD & TOBAGO
BELIZE
HONDURAS
GUATEMALA
EL SALVADOR
NICARAGUA
COSTA RICA
PANAMA

HAMILTON
SCHOOL

Canada and Greenland

CANADA

Area: 3,851,809 sq miles (9,976,139 sq km); the world's second largest country

Highest point: Mount Logan 19,849 ft (6,050 m)

Population: 26,620,000

Capital: Ottawa (pop 301,000)

Largest cities:
Toronto (3,427,000)
Montreal (2,921,000)

Official languages: English, French

Religion: Christianity (89.2%)

Main products: Motor vehicles and other manufactures, paper, minerals, farm products

Currency: Canadian Dollar

Government: Constitutional Monarchy

ST. PIERRE & MIQUELON

Area: 93 sq miles (242 sq km)

Population: 6,400

Capital: St. Pierre

Government: French territory

C D E F

Ellesmere
Island

Thule

*hurst
*land

Devon Island

*ince of
*ales
*land

Somerset
Island

Baffin Bay

Disko
Island

Godhavn

Gunnbjorn
12,139 ft

GREENLAND
(DENMARK)

Angmagssalik

Baffin
Island

Davis Strait

Frederikshaab

Cape
Farewell

40°

*ing
*illiam
*land

Melville
Peninsula

Godthaab

GREENLAND
Area: 840,000 sq miles (2,175,600
sq km)
Population: 56,000
Capital: Godthaab (pop 12,000)
Government: Self-governing part
of Denmark

RITORIES

Southampton
Island

Frobisher Bay

Hudson Strait

Ungava
Peninsula

Nain

N E W F O U N D L A N D

Eskimo Point

Labrador

Churchill

Hudson Bay

Churchill

St John's

MANITOBA

James
Bay

Anticosti
Island

Corner
Brook

Newfoundland

St Pierre &
Miquelon
(FRANCE)

Lake
Winnipeg

Fort
Albany

Fort Rupert

Q U E B E C

Glace Bay

Lake
Manitoba

O N T A R I O

Chicoutimi

NEW
BRUNSWICK

PRINCE
EDWARD ISLAND

Charlottetown

Sydney

NOVA SCOTIA

★ Winnipeg

Kenora

Timmins

Quebec

St Lawrence

Moncton

Fredericton

Saint John

Halifax

*on

Thunder Bay

Trois Rivieres

Lake Superior

Sault Ste. Marie

Sudbury

Ottawa Hull

Montreal

Cape Sable

ATLANTIC OCEAN

60°

Ottawa

Peterborough

Kingston

Lake
Huron

Oshawa

Lake
Ontario

Niagara Falls

Lake
Michigan

Kitchener

Toronto

Hamilton

London

Windsor   Lake Erie

80°

19

United States of America

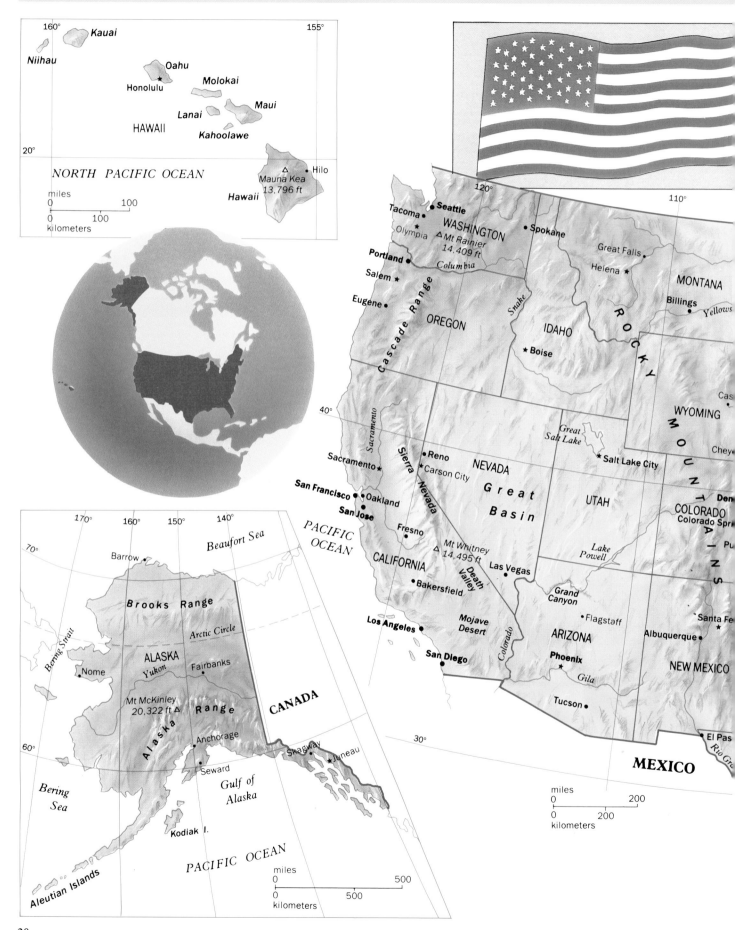

Hawaii inset:

160° 155°

Niihau
Kauai
Oahu
Honolulu
Molokai
Lanai
Maui
Kahoolawe

HAWAII

20°

NORTH PACIFIC OCEAN

Mauna Kea
13,796 ft
Hilo
Hawaii

miles
0 — 100
0 — 100
kilometers

Main map:

120° 110°

Tacoma ● **Seattle**
Olympia ★
WASHINGTON
△ Mt Rainier
14,409 ft
● Spokane
Great Falls ●
Helena ★
MONTANA
Portland ●
Columbia
Salem ★
OREGON
Snake
IDAHO
Billings ●
Yellows
Eugene ●
Cascade Range
★ Boise
ROCKY
Cas
40°
Sacramento
Great
Salt Lake
WYOMING
Sierra
● Reno
NEVADA
★ Salt Lake City
Chey
Sacramento ★
● Carson City
Great
Nevada
Basin
UTAH
Den
COLORADO
Colorado Spr
San Francisco
● Oakland
Fresno ●
Mt Whitney
△ 14,495 ft
Lake
Powell
Pu
San Jose
Las Vegas ●
CALIFORNIA
Death
Valley
PACIFIC
OCEAN
● Bakersfield
Mojave
Desert
Grand
Canyon
● Flagstaff
Santa Fe ★
Los Angeles
ARIZONA
Colorado
Albuquerque ●
San Diego
Phoenix
★
NEW MEXICO
Gila
Tucson ●
30°
MEXICO
El Pas
Rio Gra

miles
0 — 200
0 — 200
kilometers

Alaska inset:

170° 160° 150° 140°

Beaufort Sea
70°
Barrow ●
PACIFIC
OCEAN
Brooks Range
Arctic Circle
Bering Strait
ALASKA
Nome ●
Yukon
Fairbanks ●
CANADA
Mt McKinley
20,322 ft △
Range
Anchorage ●
Alaska
Skagway
Seward ●
★ Juneau
Bering
Sea
Gulf of
Alaska
60°
Kodiak I.
Aleutian Islands
PACIFIC OCEAN

miles
0 — 500
0 — 500
kilometers

UNITED STATES

Area: 3,679,192 sq miles (9,529,063 sq km); the world's fourth largest country
Highest point: Mount McKinley, Alaska, 20,322 ft (6,194 m); the highest peak in North America
Population: 249,633,000

Capital: Washington, D.C. (pop 607,000)
Largest cities:
New York City (7,323,000)
Los Angeles (3,485,000)
Chicago (2,784,000)
Houston (1,631,000)
Philadelphia (1,586,000)
Official language: English
Religion: Christianity (87.1%)

Economy: *Agriculture:* grains, oilseeds, cattle, dairy products; *Mining:* coal, copper, gold, oil, iron, nickel, silver, uranium, zinc; *Industry:* machinery and transportation equipment, chemicals, food products
Currency: U.S. Dollar
Government: Federal republic.

Northeastern States

Kentucky

Area: 40,410 sq miles (104,659 sq km)
Population: 3,699,000
Capital: Frankfort (pop 26,000)
Largest city: Louisville (pop 269,000)

West Virginia

Area: 24,232 sq miles (62,758 sq km)
Population: 1,802,000
Capital and largest city: Charleston (pop 57,000)

Virginia

Area: 40,767 sq miles (105,586 sq km)
Population: 6,217,000
Capital: Richmond (pop 203,000)
Largest city: Norfolk (pop 261,000)

Pennsylvania

Area: 46,043 sq miles (119,251 sq km)
Population: 11,925,000
Capital: Harrisburg (pop 52,000)
Largest city: Philadelphia (pop 1,586,000)

New York

Area: 52,735 sq miles (136,583 sq km)
Population: 18,045,000
Capital: Albany (pop 101,000)
Largest city: New York City (pop 7,323,000) largest in the USA

Vermont

Area: 9,614 sq miles (24,900 sq km)
Population: 565,000
Capital: Montpelier (pop 8,000)
Largest city: Burlington (pop 39,000)

New Hampshire

Area: 9,279 sq miles (24,032 sq km)
Population: 1,114,000
Capital: Concord (pop 36,000)
Largest city: Manchester (pop 100,000)

Maine

Area: 33,265 sq miles (86,156 sq km)
Population: 1,233,000
Capital: Augusta (pop 21,000)
Largest city: Portland (pop 64,000)

Massachusetts

Area: 8,284 sq miles (21,455 sq km)
Population: 6,029,000
Capital and largest city: Boston (pop 574,000)

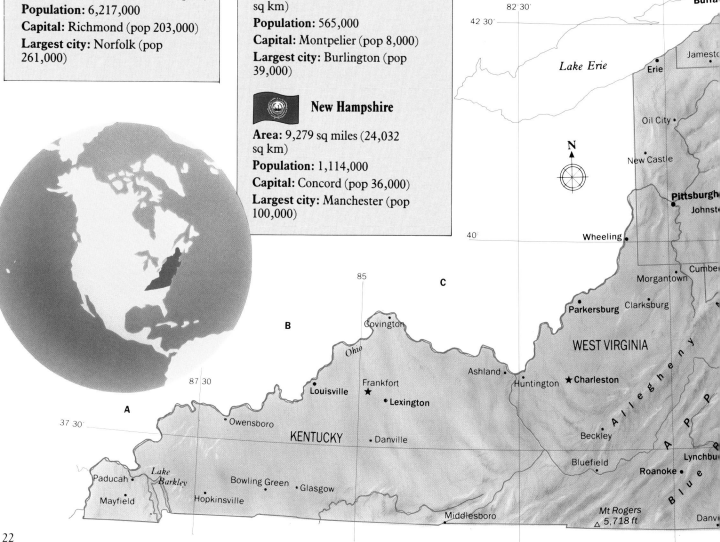

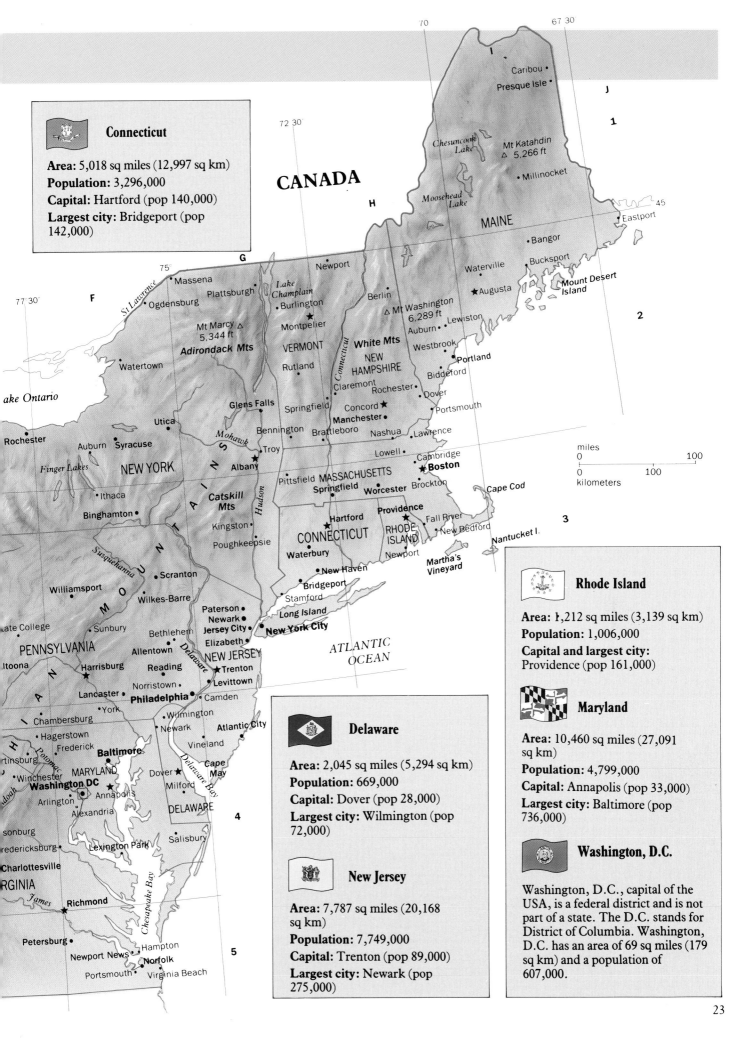

Connecticut
Area: 5,018 sq miles (12,997 sq km)
Population: 3,296,000
Capital: Hartford (pop 140,000)
Largest city: Bridgeport (pop 142,000)

CANADA

Caribou
Presque Isle

J

1

72 30'

Chesuncook Lake
Mt Katahdin
△ 5,266 ft

Millinocket

Moosehead Lake

MAINE

H

Eastport

45

Massena
Plattsburgh
Ogdensburg
Lake Champlain
Burlington
Newport

Berlin
Waterville
Bucksport
Mount Desert Island

Augusta

Bangor

G

75

St Lawrence

77 30'

F

Mt Marcy △ 5,344 ft
Adirondack Mts
Watertown

Montpelier
VERMONT
Rutland

△ Mt Washington 6,289 ft
White Mts
NEW HAMPSHIRE

Lewiston
Auburn
Westbrook
Portland

Biddeford

2

ake Ontario

Rochester

Auburn Syracuse
Finger Lakes

Utica

NEW YORK

Ithaca

Binghamton

Glens Falls

Mohawk

Troy

Albany

Catskill Mts

Hudson

Kingston

Poughkeepsie

Claremont
Springfield
Rochester
Concord ★
Manchester
Bennington Brattleboro
Nashua
Lowell
Pittsfield MASSACHUSETTS
Springfield
Worcester Brockton
Hartford Providence
CONNECTICUT RHODE
Waterbury ISLAND
Newport
New Haven
Bridgeport
Stamford
Long Island

Dover
Portsmouth
Lawrence
Cambridge
Boston

Fall River
New Bedford
Martha's Vineyard

Cape Cod

Nantucket I.

miles
0 ———— 100
0 ———— 100
kilometers

3

Susquehanna

Scranton
Wilkes-Barre

Williamsport

ate College Sunbury

PENNSYLVANIA

ltoona

Harrisburg

Lancaster

York

Chambersburg

Hagerstown
Frederick

Baltimore

MARYLAND

rtinsburg Winchester **Washington DC** ★
Arlington Annapolis
Alexandria

onsburg

redericksburg

Charlottesville

RGINIA

James **Richmond**

Petersburg

Newport News Hampton
Portsmouth Norfolk Virginia Beach

Bethlehem
Allentown
Reading
Norristown
Philadelphia

Delaware

Paterson
Newark
Jersey City
Elizabeth
★ Trenton
Levittown
Camden
Wilmington
Newark
Atlantic City
Vineland
Dover ★
Milford

NEW JERSEY

New York City

ATLANTIC OCEAN

Delaware Bay

Cape May

DELAWARE

4

Salisbury

Chesapeake Bay

5

Rhode Island
Area: 1,212 sq miles (3,139 sq km)
Population: 1,006,000
Capital and largest city: Providence (pop 161,000)

Maryland
Area: 10,460 sq miles (27,091 sq km)
Population: 4,799,000
Capital: Annapolis (pop 33,000)
Largest city: Baltimore (pop 736,000)

Washington, D.C.
Washington, D.C., capital of the USA, is a federal district and is not part of a state. The D.C. stands for District of Columbia. Washington, D.C. has an area of 69 sq miles (179 sq km) and a population of 607,000.

Delaware
Area: 2,045 sq miles (5,294 sq km)
Population: 669,000
Capital: Dover (pop 28,000)
Largest city: Wilmington (pop 72,000)

New Jersey
Area: 7,787 sq miles (20,168 sq km)
Population: 7,749,000
Capital: Trenton (pop 89,000)
Largest city: Newark (pop 275,000)

Southeastern States

 Texas

Area: 266,807 sq miles
(691,207 sq km)
Population: 17,060,000
Capital: Austin (pop 466,000)
Largest city: Houston
(pop 1,631,000)

 Oklahoma

Area: 69,956 sq miles
(181,185 sq km)
Population: 3,158,000
Capital and largest city:
Oklahoma City (pop 445,000)

 Arkansas

Area: 53,187 sq miles
(137,754 sq km)
Population: 2,362,000
Capital and largest city:
Little Rock (pop 176,000)

Louisiana

Area: 47,752 sq miles
(123,677 sq km)
Population: 4,238,000
Capital: Baton Rouge
(pop 220,000)
Largest city: New Orleans
(pop 497,000)

24

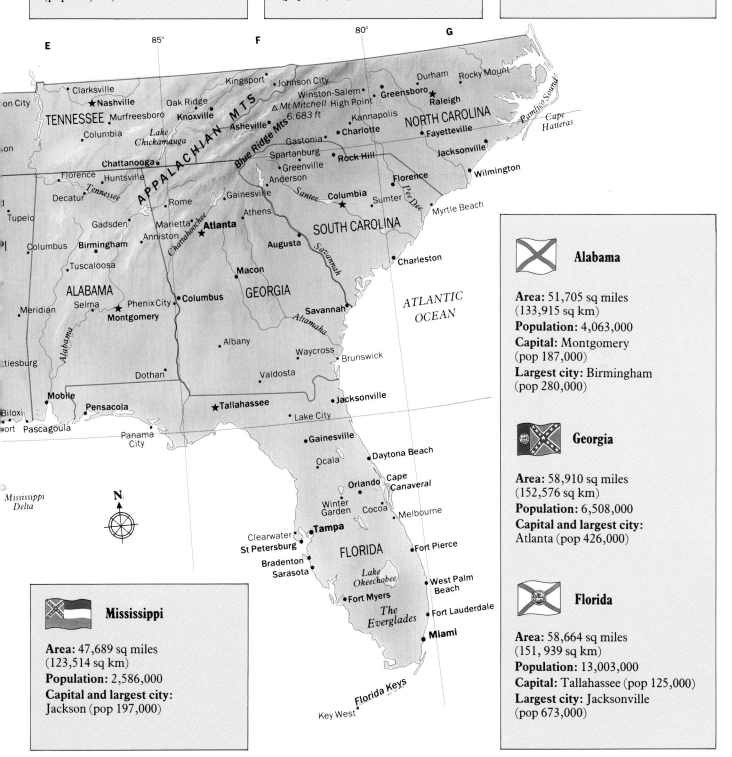

 Tennessee

Area: 42,144 sq miles
(109,152 sq km)
Population: 4,897,000
Capital: Nashville (pop 511,000)
Largest city: Memphis
(pop 610,000)

 North Carolina

Area: 52,669 sq miles
(136,412 sq km)
Population: 6,658,000
Capital: Raleigh (pop 208,000)
Largest city: Charlotte
(pop 396,000)

 South Carolina

Area: 31,113 sq miles
(80,582 sq km)
Population: 3,506,000
Capital and largest city:
Columbia (pop 98,000)

Alabama

Area: 51,705 sq miles
(133,915 sq km)
Population: 4,063,000
Capital: Montgomery
(pop 187,000)
Largest city: Birmingham
(pop 280,000)

Georgia

Area: 58,910 sq miles
(152,576 sq km)
Population: 6,508,000
Capital and largest city:
Atlanta (pop 426,000)

Florida

Area: 58,664 sq miles
(151, 939 sq km)
Population: 13,003,000
Capital: Tallahassee (pop 125,000)
Largest city: Jacksonville
(pop 673,000)

Mississippi

Area: 47,689 sq miles
(123,514 sq km)
Population: 2,586,000
Capital and largest city:
Jackson (pop 197,000)

Midwestern States

North Dakota

Area: 70,702 sq miles
(183,117 sq km)
Population: 641,000
Capital: Bismarck (pop 49,000)
Largest city: Fargo (pop 74,000)

Nebraska

Area: 77,355 sq miles
(200,349 sq km)
Population: 1,585,000
Capital: Lincoln (pop 192,000)
Largest city: Omaha (pop 336,000)

Kansas

Area: 82,277 sq miles
(213,096 sq km)
Population: 2,486,000
Capital: Topeka (pop 120,000)
Largest city: Wichita (pop 304,000)

South Dakota

Area: 77,116 sq miles
(199,730 sq km)
Population: 700,000
Capital: Pierre (pop 13,000)
Largest city: Sioux Falls
(pop 101,000)

Minnesota

Area: 86,614 sq miles
(224,329 sq km)
Population: 4,387,000
Capital: St. Paul (pop 272,000)
Largest city: Minneapolis (pop 368,000)

Iowa

Area: 56,275 sq miles
(145,752 sq km)
Population: 2,787,000
Capital and largest city:
Des Moines (pop 193,000)

 Missouri

Area: 69,697 sq miles
(180,514 sq km)
Population: 5,138,000
Capital: Jefferson City (pop 35,000)
Largest city: St. Louis
(pop 397,000)

 Wisconsin

Area: 66,215 sq miles
(171,496 sq km)
Population: 4,907,000
Capital: Madison (pop 191,000)
Largest city: Milwaukee (pop
628,000)

 Michigan

Area: 97,102 sq miles
(251,493 sq km)
Population: 9,329,000
Capital: Lansing (pop 127,000)
Largest city: Detroit (pop
1,028,000)

 Ohio

Area: 44,787 sq miles
(115,998 sq km)
Population: 10,887,000
Capital and largest city:
Columbus (pop 633,000)

 Indiana

Area: 36,413 sq miles
(94,309 sq km)
Population: 5,564,000
Capital and largest city:
Indianapolis (pop 731,000)

 Illinois

Area: 57,871 sq miles
(149,885 sq km)
Population: 11,467,000
Capital: Springfield (pop 105,000)
Largest city: Chicago (pop
2,784,000)

Western States

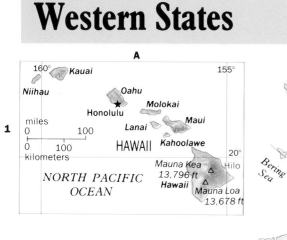

A

160° Kauai 155°

Niihau

Oahu

Molokai

Honolulu Maui

Lanai

1

miles

0   100

0   100

kilometers

HAWAII Kahoolawe

20°

Mauna Kea Hilo

13,796 ft

Hawaii

Mauna Loa

13,678 ft

NORTH PACIFIC

OCEAN

Barrow

B

Beaufort 70°

Sea

Brooks Range

Bering Strait

Nome

Arctic Circle

ALASKA

Yukon

Fairbanks

miles

0   200

Alaska △ Range

Mt McKinley

20,322 ft

Anchorage

0   200

kilometers

Bering

Sea

Seward

60°

Skagway

Gulf of

Alaska

Juneau

Kodiak

Island

Sitka

Aleutian Islands

NORTH PACIFIC

160°   OCEAN

140°

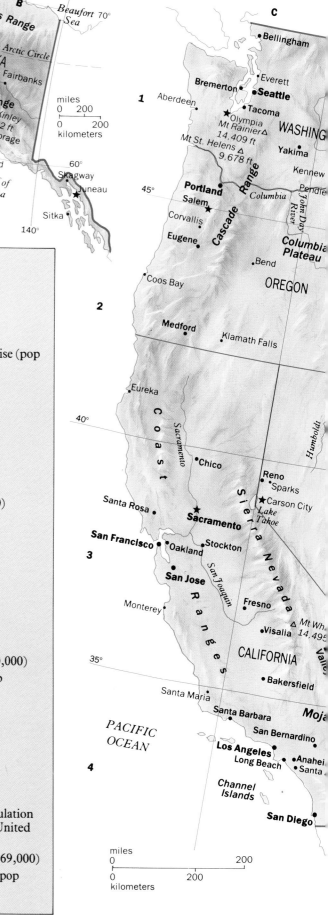

C

Bellingham

1

Aberdeen

Bremerton Everett

Seattle

Tacoma

Olympia WASHING

★ Mt Rainier △

14,409 ft

Mt St. Helens △

9,678 ft

Yakima

Kennew

Pendle

Portland

Columbia

Salem

Corvallis

John Day River

Columbia

Plateau

Eugene Bend

Coos Bay OREGON

2

Medford

Klamath Falls

Eureka

40°

Chico

Reno

Sparks

Carson City

Lake

Tahoe

Santa Rosa

Sacramento

3

San Francisco Oakland Stockton

San Jose Fresno

Monterey Visalia

Mt Wh.

14,495

35°

CALIFORNIA

Bakersfield

Santa Maria

Santa Barbara Moja

PACIFIC

OCEAN San Bernardino

Los Angeles

4 Long Beach Anahei

Santa

Channel

Islands

San Diego

miles

0   200

0   200

kilometers

Hawaii
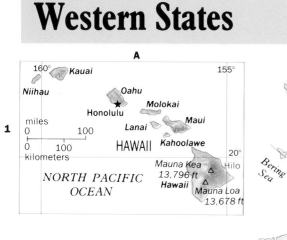

Area: 6,471 sq miles
(16,760 sq km)

Population: 1,115,000

Capital and largest city: Honolulu
(pop 365,000)

Alaska

Area: 591,004 sq miles
(1,530,693 sq km)

Population: 552,000

Capital: Juneau (pop 27,000)

Largest city: Anchorage (pop
226,000)

Washington

Area: 68,139 sq miles
(176,479 sq km)

Population: 4,888,000

Capital: Olympia (pop 34,000)

Largest city: Seattle (pop 516,000)

Idaho

Area: 83,564 sq miles
(216,430 sq km)

Population: 1,012,000

Capital and largest city: Boise (pop
126,000)

Oregon

Area: 97,073 sq miles
(251,418 sq km)

Population: 2,854,000

Capital: Salem (pop 108,000)

Largest city: Portland (pop
437,000)

Nevada

Area: 110,561 sq miles
(286,352 sq km)

Population: 1,206,000

Capital: Carson City (pop 40,000)

Largest city: Las Vegas (pop
258,000)

California

Area: 158,706 sq miles
(411,047 sq km)

Population: 29,839,000
(California has a larger population
than any other state in the United
States)

Capital: Sacramento (pop 369,000)

Largest city: Los Angeles (pop
3,485,000)

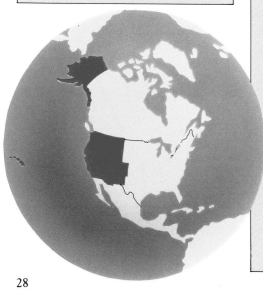

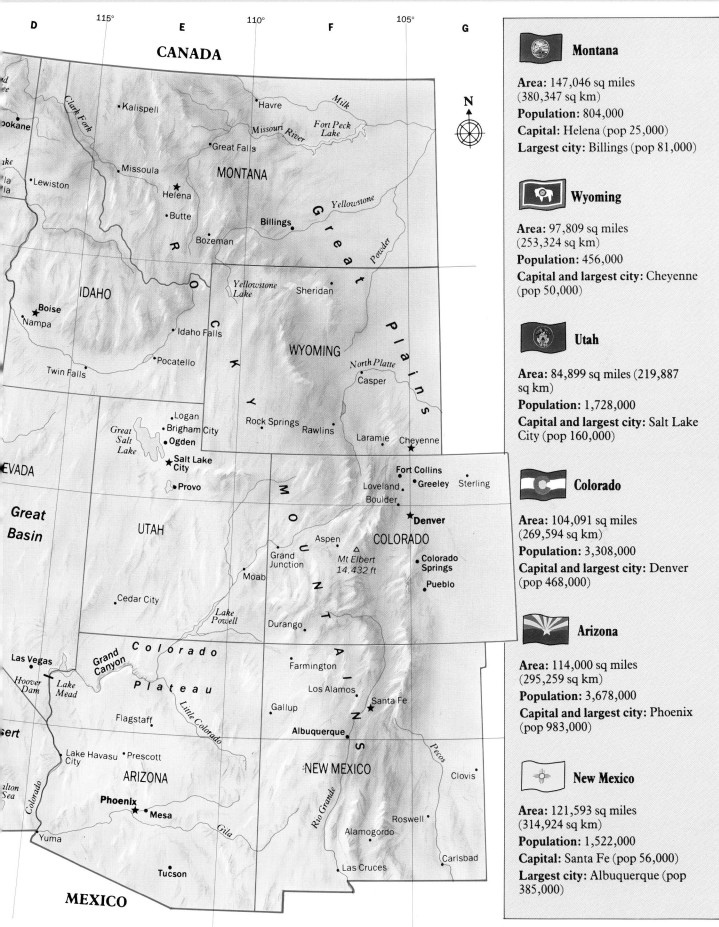

CANADA

D   115°   E   110°   F   105°   G

N

•Kalispell

•Havre

Milk

Missouri River

Fort Peck Lake

Clark Fork

•Great Falls

•Missoula

MONTANA

Helena ★

•Butte

Billings•

Bozeman•

Great Plains

Yellowstone

Powder

R
O
C
K
Y

IDAHO

Yellowstone Lake

•Sheridan

•Boise ★
•Nampa

•Idaho Falls

WYOMING

North Platte
•Casper

•Pocatello

Twin Falls•

Rock Springs• •Rawlins

•Logan
•Brigham City
•Ogden

Laramie• Cheyenne★

Great Salt Lake

★Salt Lake City

Fort Collins•
Loveland• •Greeley •Sterling
•Boulder

NEVADA

M
O
U
N
T
A
I
N
S

★•Denver

Great Basin

UTAH

•Provo

Aspen•

COLORADO

Grand Junction•

△ Mt Elbert 14,432 ft

•Colorado Springs

•Moab

•Pueblo

•Cedar City

Lake Powell

•Durango

Las Vegas•

Grand Canyon

Colorado

•Farmington

Plateau

Hoover Dam

Lake Mead

Little Colorado

•Los Alamos

•Gallup

Santa Fe★

Flagstaff•

Albuquerque•

sert

Colorado

•Lake Havasu City •Prescott

ARIZONA

NEW MEXICO

Pecos

•Clovis

alton Sea

Phoenix★ •Mesa

Roswell•

•Yuma

Gila

Rio Grande

•Alamogordo

•Carlsbad

Tucson

•Las Cruces

MEXICO

Montana

Area: 147,046 sq miles (380,347 sq km)
Population: 804,000
Capital: Helena (pop 25,000)
Largest city: Billings (pop 81,000)

Wyoming

Area: 97,809 sq miles (253,324 sq km)
Population: 456,000
Capital and largest city: Cheyenne (pop 50,000)

Utah

Area: 84,899 sq miles (219,887 sq km)
Population: 1,728,000
Capital and largest city: Salt Lake City (pop 160,000)

Colorado

Area: 104,091 sq miles (269,594 sq km)
Population: 3,308,000
Capital and largest city: Denver (pop 468,000)

Arizona

Area: 114,000 sq miles (295,259 sq km)
Population: 3,678,000
Capital and largest city: Phoenix (pop 983,000)

New Mexico

Area: 121,593 sq miles (314,924 sq km)
Population: 1,522,000
Capital: Santa Fe (pop 56,000)
Largest city: Albuquerque (pop 385,000)

29

Mexico and Central America

MEXICO

Area: 761,605 sq miles (1,972,547 sq km)

Highest point: Citlaltépetl (also called Orizaba) 18,701 ft (5,700 m)

Population: 81,485,000

Capital and largest city: Mexico City (pop 8,237,000; pop of metropolitan area 13,636,000)

Other cities:
Guadalajara (2,847,000)
Monterrey (2,522,000)
Puebla (1,055,000)

Official language: Spanish

Religion: Christianity (95.9%)

Main products: Oil, silver, machinery and other manufactures, farm products

Currency: Mexican Peso

Government: Federal republic (official name: United States of Mexico)

BELIZE

Area: 8,867 sq miles (22,965 sq km)

Population: 189,000

Capital: Belmopan (pop 3,700)

Largest city: Belize City (pop 50,000)

EL SALVADOR

Area: 8,124 sq miles
(21,041 sq km)
Population: 5,221,000
Capital and largest city: San
Salvador (pop 460,000)
Official language: Spanish
Currency: Colón

HONDURAS

Area: 43,277 sq miles
(112,088 sq km)
Population: 4,674,000
Capital and largest city:
Tegucigalpa (pop 552,000)
Currency: Lempira

GUATEMALA

Area: 42, 042 sq miles
(108,889 sq km)
Population: 9,197,000
Capital and largest city:
Guatemala City (pop 1,057,000)
Currency: Quetzal

NICARAGUA

Area: 50,193 sq miles
(130,000 sq km)
Population: 3,871,000
Capital and largest city: Managua
(pop 682,000)
Official language: Spanish
Currency: Córdoba

COSTA RICA

Area: 19,575 sq miles (50,700 sq
km)
Population: 3,015,000
Capital and largest city: San José
(pop 890,000)
Official language: Spanish
Currency: Colón

PANAMA

Area: 29,762 sq miles
(77,082 sq km)
Population: 2,148,000
Capital and largest city: Panama
City (pop 412,000)
Official language: Spanish
Currency: Balboa

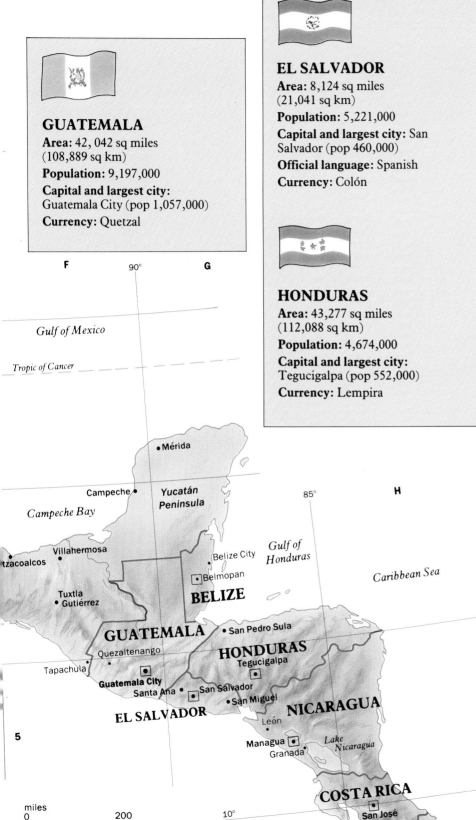

Caribbean

CUBA
Area: 42,804 sq miles (110,861 sq km)
Population: 10,603,000
Capital: Havana (pop 2,078,000)

JAMAICA
Area: 4,244 sq miles (10,991 sq km)
Population: 2,391,000
Capital: Kingston (pop 525,000)

BAHAMAS
Area: 5,380 sq miles (13,935 sq km)
Population: 253,000
Capital: Nassau (pop 169,000)

PUERTO RICO
Area: 3,435 sq miles (8,897 sq km)
Population: 3,336,000
Capital: San Juan (pop 431,000)

A

Gulf of Mexico

N

Grand Bahama I.
Freeport
Little Abaco I.
Great Abaco I.
Eleuthera I.
New Providence I.
Nassau
Andros Town
Cat I.
Andros I.
BAHAMAS
Sa Salvado
Great Exuma I.
R
C

Tropic of Cancer

Long I.
Croo
Ragged

2

Havana
Guanabacoa
Matanzas
Guines
Colón
Guane
Pinar del Rio
Santa Clara
Cienfuegos
Morón
Sancti Spiritus
Ciego de Avila
Camagüey Arch.
CUBA
Camaguey
Victoria de las Tunas
Holguin
Isle of Youth
G
r
e
a
Jardines de la Reina
Manzanillo
Pico Turquino
6,476 ft
Bayamo
Guantanam
Santiago de Cuba

20

CAYMAN ISLANDS (U.K.)
George Town
t
e
r
A
n

miles
0
200
0
200
kilometers

3

Montego Bay
JAMAICA
Mandeville
Spanish Town
Kingston
Jé
A
n

Caribbean Sea

DOMINICAN REPUBLIC
Area: 18,816 sq miles (48,734 sq km)
Population: 7,170,000
Capital and largest city: Santo Domingo (pop 1,600,000)
Official language: Spanish
Religion: Christianity
Main products: Sugar, gold, silver, coffee, cocoa
Currency: Peso

HAITI
Area: 10,714 sq miles (27,750 sq km)
Population: 5,862,000
Capital and largest city: Port-au-Prince (pop 514,000)
Official language: French, Creole
Religion: Christianity
Currency: Gourde

ANTIGUA AND BARBUDA
Area: 170 sq miles (440 sq km)
Population: 81,000
Capital: Saint John's (pop 36,000)

DOMINICA
Area: 290 sq miles (751 sq km)
Population: 82,000
Capital: Roseau (pop 22,000)

ST. CHRISTOPHER-NEVIS
Area: 101 sq miles (261 sq km)
Population: 44,000
Capital: Basseterre (pop 18,500)

ST. LUCIA
Area: 238 sq miles (616 sq km)
Population: 151,000
Capital: Castries (pop 55,000)

ST. VINCENT & THE GRENADINES
Area: 150 sq miles (388 sq km)
Population: 115,000
Capital: Kingstown (pop 19,000)

FRENCH CARIBBEAN TERRITORIES:
Guadeloupe, Martinique

NETHERLANDS TERRITORIES:
Aruba, Netherlands Antilles

BRITISH TERRITORIES:
Anguilla, Cayman Islands, Montserrat, Turks and Caicos Islands, Virgin Islands.

U.S. TERRITORY:
Virgin Islands

C   70'

ins I.
Mayaguana I.
TURKS & CAICOS ISLANDS (U.K.)
reat
gua I.   Grand Turk
thew Town

D   ATLANTIC
         OCEAN   65

E   F

Cap-Haïtien   Puerto Plata
naïves   Santiago   DOMINICAN
         La Vega
St Marc   REPUBLIC
Port-au-Prince   Azua   La Romana
HAITI   Santo
Cayes   Jacmel   Barahona   Domingo

VIRGIN
ISLANDS
(U.S.) (U.K.)   ANGUILLA (U.K.)
Arecibo San Juan
         Road Town   St. Martin
Mayaguez Ponce   Charlotte
                  Amalie   ANTIGUA
PUERTO RICO   AND
(U.S.)   Basseterre   BARBUDA
         ST CHRISTOPHER-   St John's
                  NEVIS   MONTSERRAT (U.K.)
                           Plymouth
I l e s   GUADELOUPE (Fr.)
                           Basse Terre
                                    DOMINICA
                           Roseau

                                 60

                           15

L e s s e r   MARTINIQUE (Fr.)
                Fort-de-France
A
n
t   Castries   ST LUCIA
i
l   Kingstown   BARBADOS
l   Bridgetown
e
s   ST VINCENT
           & THE
           GRENADINES
4
St George's
         GRENADA   Tobago
                  Scarborough
                  TRINIDAD AND
Port of Spain   TOBAGO
San Fernando   Trinidad

                           10

GRENADA
Area: 133 sq miles (344 sq km)
Population: 100,000
Capital: St. George's (pop 30,000)

BARBADOS
Area: 166 sq miles (431 sq km)
Population: 257,000
Capital: Bridgetown (pop 7,400)

NETHERLANDS ANTILLES

Aruba   Bonaire
   Curaçao
      Willemstad

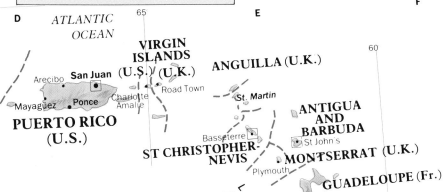

TRINIDAD AND TOBAGO
Area: 1,981 sq miles (5,130 sq km)
Population: 1,233,000
Capital: Port of Spain (pop 300,000)

South America

South America is the fourth largest continent. It includes Brazil, a country that is larger than Australia. Much of the continent has a warm climate and forests cover large areas of the north. Deserts border the coasts of west-central South America. Patagonia, in Argentina, is a dry, cold region.

The Andes Mountains, the world's longest mountain range, contains Aconcagua, South America's highest peak. The longest river is the Amazon.

South America includes 12 independent countries, French Guiana, which is ruled as part of France, and the Falkland Islands, which are ruled by Britain. South America has about 300 million people. A few people are wealthy, but the great majority are poor.

South America (Physical)

PACIFIC OCEAN

San Félix I.
(Chile) ● San Ambrosio I.
(Chile)

Juan Fernández Is. (Chile)

CHILE

Antofagasta ●

La Serena ●

Viña del Mar ●
Valparaíso ●
Rancagua ●
Talca ●
Talcahuano ●
Concepción ●
Temuco ●
Valdivia ●
Osorno ●
Puerto Montt ●

Chillán ●

Santiago ⊡
△ Aconcagua 22.834 ft
Mendoza ●
San Juan ●
Río Cuarto
Córdoba ●
Salta ●
San Miguel de
Tucumán ●
Santiago
del Estero ●

ANDES MOUNTAINS

Tropic of Capricorn

D e s e r t

CHILE

Gran Chaco

PARAGUAY

Concepción ●
Asunción ⊡
Posadas ●
Resistencia ●
Corrientes ●

Pilcomayo

Paraná

Uruguay

Santa Fe ●
Paraná ●
Rosario ●

Buenos Aires ⊡
La Plata ●

ARGENTINA

P a m p a

Tandil ●

Bahía Blanca ●

Colorado

Negro

P a t a g o n i a

Chubut

Deseado

Comodoro Rivadavia ●

Strait of Magellan

Punta Arenas ●
Tierra del Fuego
Ushuaia ●

Cape Horn

Mar del Plata ●

Montevideo ⊡
URUGUAY

Paysandú ●
Salto ●
Rivera ●

Bagé ●
Pelotas ●

Uruguaiana ●
Santa María ●

Pôrto Alegre ●

Passo Fundo ●
Ponta Grossa ●

Presidente
Prudente ●

Sorocaba ●
Bauru ●
Campinas ●
São Paulo ●
Santos ●
Volta Redonda ●
Rio de Janeiro ●
Campos ●

Curitiba ●
Blumenau ●
Florianópolis ●

SOUTH
ATLANTIC
OCEAN

miles
0 —————— 500
0 —————— 500
kilometers

Falkland Islands (U.K.)

● Stanley

30°

40°

50°

5

6

7

8

37

South America (Political)

COLOMBIA
Area: 439,737 sq miles (1,138,914 sq km)
Population: 32,978,000
Capital and largest city: Bogotá (pop 4,820,000)
Currency: Colombian Peso

VENEZUELA
Area: 352,145 sq miles (912,050 sq km)
Population: 19,735,000
Capital and largest city: Caracas (pop 1,290,000)
Currency: Bolivar

ECUADOR
Area: 109,484 sq miles (283,561 sq km)
Population: 10,782,000
Capital: Quito (1,234,000)
Currency: Sucre

PERU
Area: 496,225 sq miles (1,285,216 sq km)
Population: 22,332,000
Capital and largest city: Lima (pop 5,659,000)
Currency: Sol

BOLIVIA
Area: 424,165 sq miles (1,098,581 sq km)
Population: 7,322,000
Capital and largest city: La Paz (pop 1,050,000)
Currency: Boliviano

CHILE
Area: 292,258 sq miles (756,945 sq km)
Population: 13,173,000
Capital and largest city: Santiago (pop 5,134,000)
Currency: Chilean Peso

Caracas

VENEZUELA

Bogotá

COLOMBIA

Quito

ECUADOR

PERU

Lima

La Paz

BOLIVI

CHILE

Santiago

GUYANA
Area: 83,000 sq miles (214,969 sq km)
Population: 756,000
Capital: Georgetown (150,000)
Currency: Guyana Dollar

SURINAM
Area: 63,037 sq miles (163,265 sq km)
Population: 411,000
Capital: Paramaribo (192,000)
Currency: Surinam Guilder

FRENCH GUIANA
Area: 34,749 sq miles (90,000 sq km)
Population: 117,000
Capital: Cayenne (42,000)
Currency: Franc

BRAZIL
Area: 3,286,488 sq miles (8,511,965 sq km)
Population: 150,368,000
Capital: Brasilia (pop 1,566,000)
Largest cities: São Paulo (16,800,000 metropolitan area) Rio de Janeiro (11,100,000) Belo Horizonte (3,400,000)
Official language: Portuguese
Currency: Cruzeiro

PARAGUAY
Area: 157,048 sq miles (406,752 sq km)
Population: 4,279,000
Capital and largest city: Asunción (pop 608,000)
Official language: Spanish
Currency: Guarani

ARGENTINA
Area: 1,068,302 sq miles (2,766,889 sq km)
Highest point: Aconcagua 22,831 ft (6,960 m)
Population: 32,880,000
Capital and largest city: Buenos Aires (pop 2,923,000; metropolitan area 9,968,000)
Official language: Spanish
Religion: Christianity
Currency: Argentine Peso

URUGUAY
Area: 68,037 sq miles (176,215 sq km)
Population: 3,033,000
Capital and largest city: Montevideo (pop 1,312,000)
Currency: New Peso

FALKLAND ISLANDS (U.K.)
Area: 4,700 sq miles (12,173 sq km)
Population: 2,000
Capital: Stanley

Europe

Europe is the second smallest continent; only Australia is smaller. It contains parts of the former Soviet Union including Belarus, Moldova, Ukraine, Estonia, Latvia, Lithuania, and part of the Russian Federation, the world's largest country and the only country located in more than one continent.

The highest peak in Europe is Mount Elbrus in the Caucasus Mountains, which form part of the border between Europe and Asia. The longest river, the Volga, is in the Russian Federation and flows into the Caspian Sea.

Europe also contains the world's smallest country, Vatican City, which is situated in Rome, the capital of Italy.

Europe's population of about 700 million is greater than that of any other continent except Asia.

France, Belgium, and Switzerland

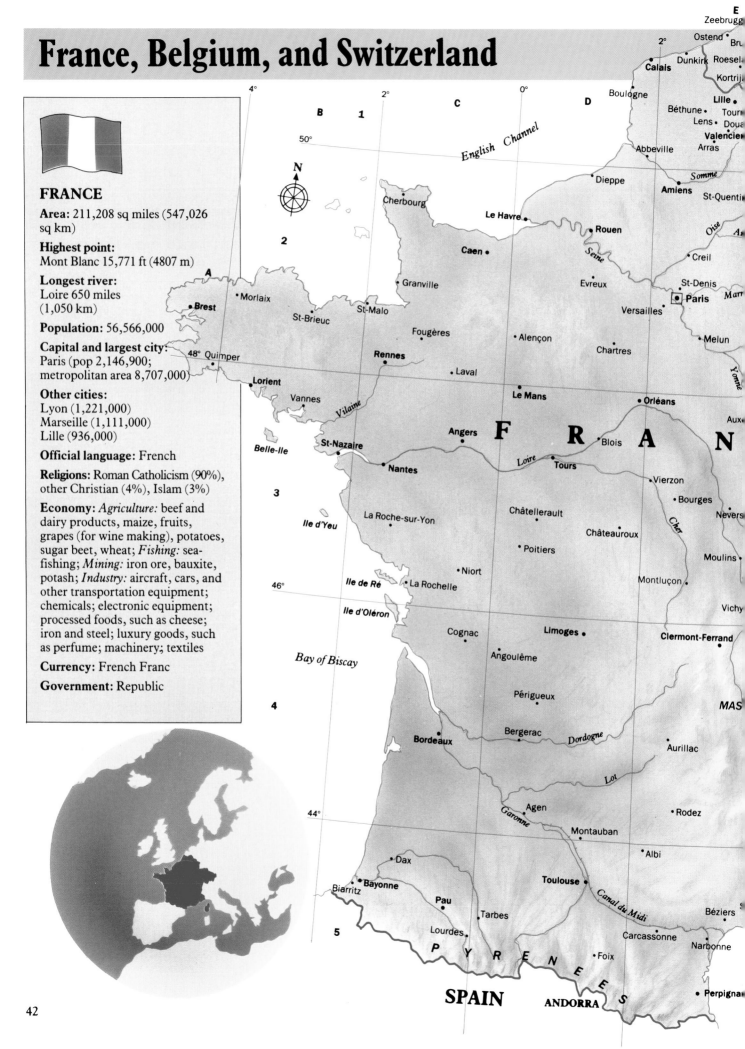

FRANCE

Area: 211,208 sq miles (547,026 sq km)

Highest point: Mont Blanc 15,771 ft (4807 m)

Longest river: Loire 650 miles (1,050 km)

Population: 56,566,000

Capital and largest city: Paris (pop 2,146,900; metropolitan area 8,707,000)

Other cities:
Lyon (1,221,000)
Marseille (1,111,000)
Lille (936,000)

Official language: French

Religions: Roman Catholicism (90%), other Christian (4%), Islam (3%)

Economy: *Agriculture:* beef and dairy products, maize, fruits, grapes (for wine making), potatoes, sugar beet, wheat; *Fishing:* sea-fishing; *Mining:* iron ore, bauxite, potash; *Industry:* aircraft, cars, and other transportation equipment; chemicals; electronic equipment; processed foods, such as cheese; iron and steel; luxury goods, such as perfume; machinery; textiles

Currency: French Franc

Government: Republic

N

4°   2°   0°

2°

50°

English Channel

B 1   C   D

Zeebrugg
Ostend   Bru
Calais   Dunkirk   Roesel
Boulogne   Kortrij
Lille   Tou
Béthune   Doua
Lens   Valencie
Abbeville   Arras
Somme
Dieppe
Amiens   St-Quenti
Rouen   Oise   A
Le Havre
Caen   Seine   Creil
Granville   Evreux   St-Denis
Marr
Paris
Versailles
Cherbourg
Morlaix
Brest
St-Brieuc   St-Malo
Quimper   Fougères   Alençon   Chartres   Melun
48°   Rennes   Laval   Yonne
Lorient   Le Mans
Vannes   Vilaine   Angers   Orléans
St-Nazaire   Blois   Aux
Belle-Ile   F   R   A   N
Nantes   Loire   Tours
3   Vierzon
La Roche-sur-Yon   Bourges
Ile d'Yeu   Châtellerault   Châteauroux   Nevers
Poitiers   Moulins
Niort   Montluçon
46°   Ile de Ré   La Rochelle   Vichy
Ile d'Oléron
Limoges   Clermont-Ferrand
Cognac
Angoulême
Bay of Biscay
Périgueux
4   MAS
Bordeaux   Bergerac   Dordogne
Aurillac
Lot   Rodez
44°   Agen   Garonne
Montauban
Dax   Albi
Bayonne   Toulouse   Canal du Midi
Biarritz
Pau   Béziers
Tarbes
5   Lourdes   Carcassonne
Foix   Narbonne
P Y R E N E E S   Perpigna

SPAIN   **ANDORRA**

42

F

Turnhout
• Antwerp
nt
Aalst • Mechelen   Genk
· Hasselt
☐ Brussels
ELGIUM   • Liège
ons   • Verviers
Charleroi · Namur
beuge
Reims   6°

Charleville-Mézières

G

LUXEMBOURG
☐ Luxembourg

Esch-sur-Alzette
Thionville
ernay   Metz   · Forbach
• St-Dizier   Nancy
• Troyes   **Strasbourg**
St-Dié
Chaumont   Colmar   Rhine

8°   **GERMANY**   10°

H
Schaffhausen • Konstanz   Lake
Constance
Mulhouse   Baden Winterthur
Belfort   • St Gallen
Montbéliard •   **Basel** • Zürich
Saône   Olten
• Dijon   **Besançon**   Solothurn   **LIECHTENSTEIN**
La Chaux-de-   **Luzern**   ☐ Vaduz
Fonds   · Biel   Chur
E   Neuchâtel   ☐ **Bern**
Lake   Fribourg   · Thun   Davos
Neuchâtel   St Moritz
Châlon-sur-Saône   Jura Mts   Lausanne   **SWITZERLAND**
• Mâcon   Lake   Montreux   Brig   Locarno
Geneva   • Lugano
Bourg-en-Bresse   • **Geneva**   Zermatt
• Roanne   Annecy   Matterhorn
Lyon • Villeurbanne   Mont Blanc   14,692 ft
15,771 ft
St-Étienne   • Vienne   Chambéry
'uy   Isère   Grenoble   **ITALY**
• Valence
Rhône   • Montélimar

AUSTRIA

MEDITERRANEAN SEA

Alès
• Avignon
• Nîmes   9°
tpellier · Arles   • Bastia
Nice • **MONACO**
• Aix-en-Provence   Cannes   Mt Cinto
8,891 ft
Marseille •   • St-Tropez
CORSICA   42°
Toulon   Ajaccio
ulf of
ion

BELGIUM

Area: 11,781 sq miles (30,513 sq km)

Population: 9,886,000

Capital: Brussels (pop 970,000)

Official languages: Dutch, French

Economy: Chemicals, coal, dairy products, meat, steel, textiles

Currency: Belgian Franc

Government: Monarchy

LUXEMBOURG

Area: 998 sq miles (2,586 sq km)

Population: 379,000

Capital: Luxembourg (pop 86,000)

Official languages: French, German, Luxemburgish

Economy: Mainly manufacturing

Government: Monarchy

SWITZERLAND

Area: 15,943 sq miles (41,293 sq km)

Population: 6,541,000

Capital: Bern (pop 299,000)

Official languages: German, French, Italian

Economy: Manufacturing, including watches and precision instruments; agriculture, especially dairy products; tourism and banking

Currency: Swiss Franc

Government: Federal Republic

MONACO

Area: 0.7 sq miles (1.9 sq km)

Population: 29,000

Capital: Monaco (pop 1,200)

Government: Principality

LIECHTENSTEIN

Area: 61 sq miles (157 sq km)

Population: 29,000

Capital: Valduz (pop 4,900)

Government: Principality

---

miles
0   50
0   50
kilometers

43

British Isles

UNITED KINGDOM

Area: 93,643 sq miles (242,534 sq km)

Highest point: Ben Nevis, Scotland, 4,406 ft (1,343 m)

Population: 57,411,000

Capital and largest city: London (pop 6,378,000)

Other cities:
Birmingham (935,000)
Leeds (674,000)
Glasgow (645,000)
Sheffield (500,000)

Official language: English

Religions: Protestant (49.1%), Roman Catholic (29.6%), other Christians (8.4%), Jewish (2.7%), Muslim (1.9%), other (8.3%)

Economy: *Agriculture:* wheat, barley, potatoes, sugar beet, livestock, dairy products; *Fishing:* wet fish, shellfish; *Mining:* coal, oil and natural gas, tin, iron ore; *Industry:* machinery and transportation equipment, metals, food processing, paper

Currency: Pound sterling

Government: Monarchy, whose official name is the United Kingdom of Great Britain and Northern Ireland (or U.K.) Great Britain consists of England, Scotland, and Wales.

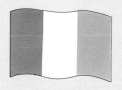

REPUBLIC OF IRELAND

Area: 27,137 sq miles (70,284 sq km)

Highest point: Carrauntoohill, 3,414 ft (1,041 m)

Population: 3,509,000 ·

Capital and largest city: Dublin (pop 503,000)

Official languages: Irish, English

Religions: Roman Catholic 93.1%, Church of Ireland (Protestant) 2.8%

Main products: Machinery and transportation equipment, food

Currency: Irish Pound (Punt)

Government: Republic

Countries in the U.K.
England
Area: 50,378 sq miles (130,478 sq km)

Population: 47,837,000

Capital: London (pop 6,378,000)

Northern Ireland
Area: 5,452 sq miles (14,121 sq km)

Population: 1,590,000

Capital: Belfast (pop 281,000)

Scotland
Area: 29,794 sq miles (77,167 sq km)

Population: 5,102,000

Capital: Edinburgh (pop 421,000)

Wales
Area: 8,019 sq miles (20,768 sq km)

Population: 2,882,000

Capital: Cardiff (pop 273,000)

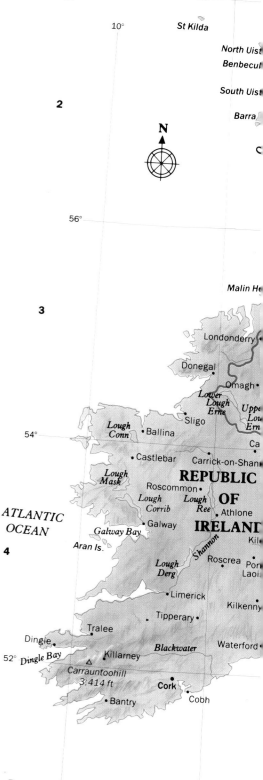

6

Spain and Portugal

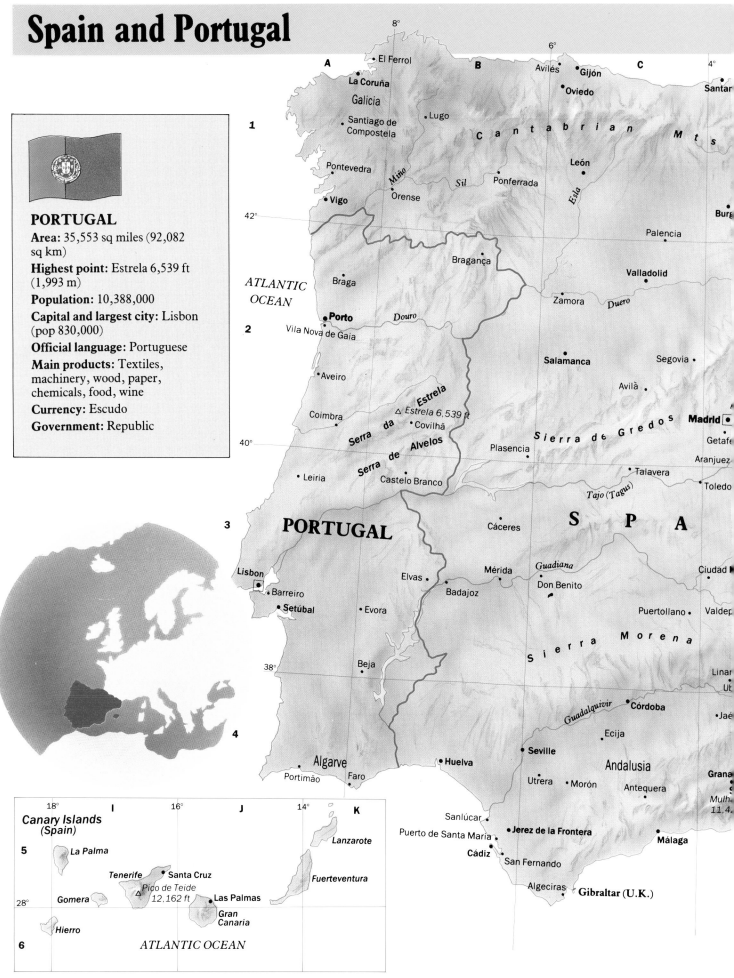

8°

6°

4°

A · El Ferrol

La Coruña

Galicia

B · Avilés · Gijón

· Oviedo

C

· Santar

1 · Santiago de Compostela

· Lugo

C a n t a b r i a n   M t s

· Pontevedra

· León

· Ponferrada

Esla

Burg

42° · Vigo

Miño

Sil

· Orense

· Palencia

ATLANTIC OCEAN

· Braga

· Bragança

· Valladolid

· Zamora

Duero

2 · Porto

Douro

Vila Nova de Gaia

· Salamanca

· Segovia

· Avilà

Madrid ·

· Aveiro

Sierra   de   Gredos

Getafe

· Coimbra

Estrela

△ Estrela 6,539 ft

· Covilhã

40° · Plasencia

Aranjuez

Serra   da

Serra   de   Alvelos

· Talavera

· Toledo

· Leiria

· Castelo Branco

Tajo (Tagus)

3 **PORTUGAL**

· Cáceres

S   P   A

· Mérida

Guadiana

Ciudad

Lisbon

· Elvas

· Badajoz

· Don Benito

□

· Barreiro

· Evora

· Puertollano

· Valdep

· Setúbal

Sierra   Morena

38° · Beja

Linar

Ub

Guadalquivir

· Córdoba

· Jaé

· Ecija

4 Algarve

· Seville

Andalusia

Grana

Portimão

· Faro

· Huelva

· Utrera

· Morón

· Antequera

Mulh 11,4.

· Sanlúcar

· Jerez de la Frontera

· Málaga

Puerto de Santa Maria ·

· Cádiz

San Fernando

· Algeciras · **Gibraltar (U.K.)**

PORTUGAL

Area: 35,553 sq miles (92,082 sq km)

Highest point: Estrela 6,539 ft (1,993 m)

Population: 10,388,000

Capital and largest city: Lisbon (pop 830,000)

Official language: Portuguese

Main products: Textiles, machinery, wood, paper, chemicals, food, wine

Currency: Escudo

Government: Republic

18°

16°

14°

I

J

K

Canary Islands (Spain)

5 · *La Palma*

△

· Santa Cruz

Tenerife

Lanzarote

Pico de Teide 12,162 ft

Fuerteventura

28° · *Gomera*

· Las Palmas

· *Hierro*

Gran Canaria

6 *ATLANTIC OCEAN*

46

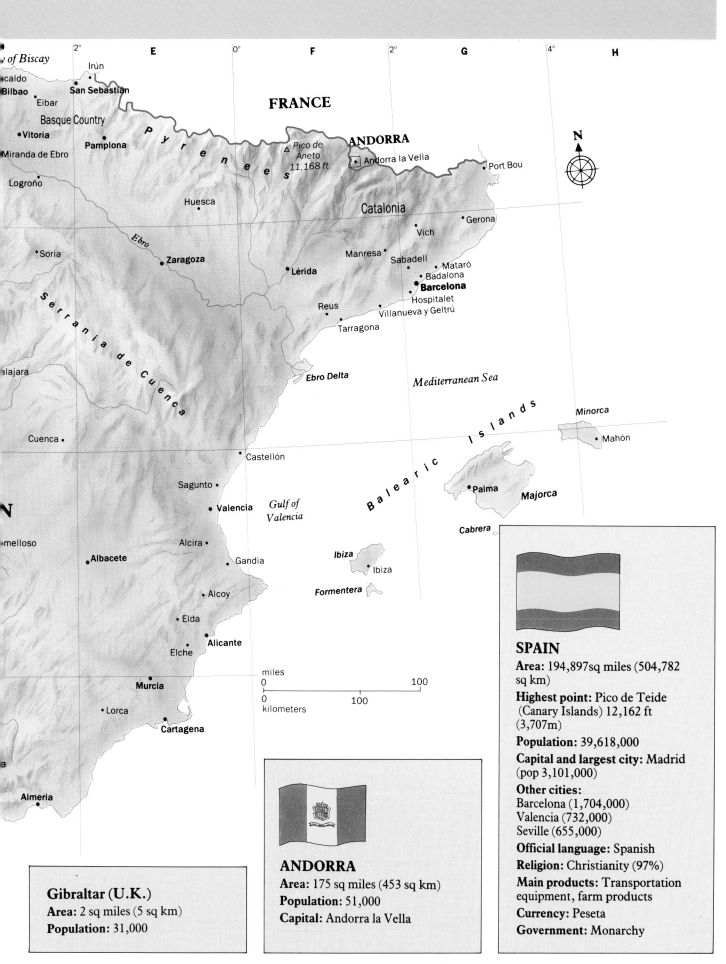

of Biscay

Irún

caldo
Bilbao • San Sebastián
• Eibar

Basque Country

FRANCE

ANDORRA

• **Vitoria**
Pamplona

P y r e n e e s

△ Pico de
Aneto
11,168 ft

Andorra la Vella

• Port Bou

Miranda de Ebro

Logroño

Huesca

Catalonia

• Gerona

• Soria

E b r o

• **Zaragoza**

Vich

Manresa   Sabadell
• **Lérida**   • Mataró
• Badalona
● **Barcelona**
Hospitalet

Reus •
Villanueva y Geltrú

Tarragona

S e r r a n i a   d e   C u e n c a

alajara

Ebro Delta

Mediterranean Sea

B a l e a r i c   I s l a n d s

Minorca

• Mahón

Cuenca •

N

melloso

Albacete

Sagunto •

• **Valencia**

*Gulf of
Valencia*

Alcira •

Gandia

Ibiza

Ibiza

Formentera

Palma

Majorca

Cabrera

• Alcoy

• Elda

Elche   **Alicante**

Murcia

• Lorca

Cartagena

miles
0   100

0   100
kilometers

N

SPAIN
Area: 194,897sq miles (504,782 sq km)
Highest point: Pico de Teide (Canary Islands) 12,162 ft (3,707m)
Population: 39,618,000
Capital and largest city: Madrid (pop 3,101,000)
Other cities:
Barcelona (1,704,000)
Valencia (732,000)
Seville (655,000)
Official language: Spanish
Religion: Christianity (97%)
Main products: Transportation equipment, farm products
Currency: Peseta
Government: Monarchy

Almeria

ANDORRA
Area: 175 sq miles (453 sq km)
Population: 51,000
Capital: Andorra la Vella

Gibraltar (U.K.)
Area: 2 sq miles (5 sq km)
Population: 31,000

Northwestern Europe

A · 24° · 20° **B** 16° **C** **D** 8° **E** 70° 12° **F** 16° **1** **G** 20° **H**

Arctic Circle

Hammerf

Norwegian Sea

Tromsø

1

Isafjördhur

Siglufjördhur

Lofoten Islands

Harstad

L a p l a

66°

Akureyri

Narvik

Kebnekaise
6,965 ft

Kiruna

ICELAND

Bodø

Mi

Gällivare

2

Vatnajökull
(Glacier)

Seydhisfjördhur

Reykjavik

Hofn

Arctic Circle

Lule

Keflavik

Hafnarfjördhur

△ Hvannadalshnúkur
6,952 ft

66°

Boden

Skellefte

Luleå

Heimaey I. ▫

2

Surtsey I. ○

Skellefteå

3

Ume

Faroe Is.
(Denmark)

Namsos

Umeå

Gulf of Bothnia

62°

Tórshavn

Steinkjer

Kokko

Örnsköldsvik

Trondheim

Ålesund

7°

Molde

Östersund

Härnösand

Vaasa

Sundsvall

62°

NORWAY

△ Glittertind
8,104 ft

Jostedal
Glacier

Ljungan

ATLANTIC
OCEAN

Sogne Fiord

Lillenhammer

Klar

SWEDEN

Pori

Tampere

Rauma

4

Bergen

Gjøvik

Glåma

Falun

Gävle

Hämeenlinn

Hardanger
Plateau

Ringerike

Hamar

Börlänge

Sandviken

Haugesund

Drammen

▫ Oslo

Åland
Islands

Turku

Stavanger

Skien

Moss

Uppsala

Var

Karlstad

Västerås

Espoo
Hel

58°

Kristiansand

Fredrikstad

Arendal

Lake
Vänern

Örebro

Eskilstuna

▫ Stockholm

Lake
Vättern

Norrköping

Baltic Sea

North Sea

Skagerrak

Uddevalla

Linköping

5

Frederikshaven

Borås

Göteborg

Jönköping

Visby

Gotland

Holstebro

Ålborg

Jutland

Kattegat

Växjö

Herning

Randers

Halmstad

Kalmar

Öland

DENMARK

Århus

Helsingborg

Esbjerg

Copenhagen

Kolding

Odense

Slagelse

Lund

Kristianstad

Karlskrona

GERMANY

Malmö

Bornholm

miles
0 _____ 100

0 ____ 100
kilometers

N

RUSSIA

FINLAND

ICELAND
Area: 39,769 sq miles (103,000 sq km)

Population: 256,000

Capital: Reykjavik (pop 97,000)

Main export: Fish and fish products

Currency: Icelandic Króna

Government: Republic

NORWAY
Area: 125,182 sq miles (324,219 sq km)

Population: 4,246,000

Capital: Oslo (pop 458,000)

Main export: Oil and natural gas

Currency: Krone

Government: Monarchy

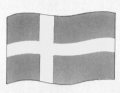

SWEDEN
Area: 173,732 sq miles (449,964 sq km)

Population: 8,529,000

Capital: Stockholm (pop 672,000)

Main exports: Machinery and transportation equipment, wood and wood pulp, chemicals

Currency: Swedish Krona

Government: Monarchy

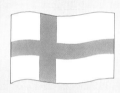

FINLAND
Area: 130,129 sq miles (337,032 sq km)

Population: 4,978,000

Capital: Helsinki (pop 491,000)

Main exports: Metal products and machinery, paper, wood and wood products

Currency: Markka

Government: Republic

DENMARK
Area: 16,629 sq miles (43,069 sq km) not including the Faroe Islands and Greenland

Population: 5,139,000

Capital: Copenhagen (pop 618,000)

Main exports: Machinery and instruments, food products

Currency: Danish Krone

Government: Monarchy

Germany and North-Central Europe

North Sea

Frisian Islands

Leeuwarden

Wilhelmshaven

Flensburg

Kiel

Neumünster

Stralsund

Baltic Sea

G

Słupsk

Koszalin

NETHERLANDS

Haarlem

Groningen

IJsselmeer

Oldenburg

Bremerhaven

Bremen

Lübeck

Hamburg

Schwerin

Wismar

Rostock

Szczecin

Pila

Bydgoszcz

Inowrocł.

The Hague

Amsterdam

Utrecht

Enschede

Osnabrück

Hanover

Weser

Braunschweig

Berlin

Potsdam

Warta

Poznań

Rotterdam

Arnhem

Bielefeld

Salzgitter

Magdeburg

Oder

Breda

Eindhoven

Münster

GERMANY

Halberstadt

Harz Mts

Dessau

Cottbus

Neisse

Kalisz

Maastricht

Maas

Duisburg

Dortmund

Essen

Krefeld

Düsseldorf

Wuppertal

Kassel

Halle

Leipzig

Görlitz

Legnica

Wrocław

BELGIUM

Aachen

Cologne

Bonn

Erfurt

Gera

Dresden

Chemnitz

Sudeten Mts

Wałbrzych

Opole

Koblenz

Giessen

Thuringian Forest

Zwickau

Plauen

Usti nad Labem

Liberec

Eifel

Mosel

Wiesbaden

Frankfurt am Main

Offenbach

Schweinfurt

Main

Bamberg

Ore Mts

Kladno

Hradec Králové

CZECH

Prague

Ostra

Trier

Mainz

Darmstadt

Würzburg

Pardubice

REPUBLIC

Olomouc

Mannheim

Heidelberg

Nuremberg

Plzeň

Pribram

FRANCE

Saarbrücken

Karlsruhe

Heilbronn

Regensburg

Bohemian Forest

České Budějovice

Jihlava

Brno

Znojmo

Rhine

Stuttgart

Danube

Black Forest

Freiburg

Ravensburg

Ulm

Augsburg

Munich

Inn

Krems

Wels

Linz

Steyr

St. Pölten

Vienna

Bratislava

SWITZERLAND

Lake Constance

Dornbirn

Alps

Innsbruck

AUSTRIA

Leoben

Gross Glockner 12,461 ft

Enns

Wiener Neustadt

Lake Neusiedler

Győr

Szombathely

Székesfehérvár

ITALY

Salzburg

Graz

Mur

Lake Balaton

Villach

Klagenfurt

Drava

Nagykanizsa

SLOVENIA

P

CROATIA

NETHERLANDS

Area: 15,770 sq miles (40,844 sq km)

Population: 14,934,000

Capital: Amsterdam (pop 695,000)

Official language: Dutch

Main exports: Machinery and transportation equipment, food, chemicals, mineral fuels, including natural gas, metals and metal products

Currency: Guilder

Government: Monarchy

E   N   22°   F

RUSSIA   LITHUANIA

k

• Elblag

Olsztyn •

Łomza •

Białystok •

oclawek •

Vistula

• Warsaw

Bug

• Siedlce

BELARUS

OLAND

• Łódź

• Piotrków   Puławy •

Radom •   • Lublin

• Kielce

zęstochowa   Zamość •

ów

ice   *Vistula*   San

• Kraków   Rzeszów •   Jarosław •

Przemysl •

arpathian Mts

△ *Gerlachovka Stit*
8,711 ft

OVAK REPUBLIC

• Košice   UKRAINE

• Miskolc

Tisza   Debrecen •

lapest

NGARY

skémét   Békéscsaba •

Hódmezóvásárhely •   ROMANIA

zeged •

GOSLAVIA

miles
0   100
0   100
kilometers

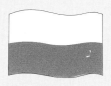

POLAND

Area: 120,725 sq miles (312,677 sq km)

Population: 38,064,000

Capital: Warsaw (pop 1,651,000)

Main exports: Machinery and transportation equipment

Currency: Zloty

Government: Republic

GERMANY

Area: 137,744 sq miles (356,755 sq km)

Population: 79,070,000

Capital: Berlin (pop 3,410,000)

Other cities:
Hamburg (1,603,000)
Munich, or München (1,212,000)
Cologne, or Köln (937,000)
Frankfurt am Main (625,000)

Official language: German

Religion: Protestant (43%), Roman Catholic (35%)

Economy: *Agriculture:* barley, wheat, rye, potatoes, sugar beet; *Fishing:* cod, herring; *Mining:* coal, lignite, iron, potash; *Industry:* machinery and transportation equipment, motor vehicles, chemicals and chemical products

Currency: Mark

Government: Republic

CZECH REPUBLIC

Area: 30,450 sq miles (78,864 sq km)

Population: 10,404,000

Capital: Prague (pop 1,211,000)

SLOVAK REPUBLIC

Area: 18,933 sq miles (49,035 sq km)

Population: 4,991,000

Capital: Bratislava (pop 441,000)

AUSTRIA

Area: 32,374 sq miles (83,849 sq km)

Population: 7,623,000

Capital: Vienna (pop 1,483,000)

Main exports: Machinery and transportation equipment

Currency: Schilling

Government: Republic

HUNGARY

Area: 35,919 sq miles (93,030 sq km)

Population: 10,437,000

Capital: Budapest (pop 2,114,000)

Main exports: Machinery and transportation equipment

Currency: Forint

Government: Republic

Italy and Southeastern Europe

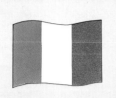

ITALY

Area: 116,304 sq miles (301,225 sq km)

Population: 57,512,000

Capital: Rome (pop 2,816,000)

Other large cities:
Milan (1,464,000)
Naples (1,203,000)
Turin (1,012,000)

Official language: Italian

Religion: Roman Catholic (90%)

Economy: *Agriculture:* fruits, vegetables, grains; *Mining:* oil and natural gas; *Industry:* machinery and transportation equipment, textiles, iron and steel

Currency: Lira

Government: Republic

VATICAN CITY (in Rome)

Area: 109 acres (44 hectares)

Population: 1,000

SAN MARINO

Area: 24 sq miles (61 sq km)

Population: 23,000

Capital: San Marino (pop 4,500)

MALTA

Area: 122 sq miles (316 sq km)

Population: 353,000

Capital: Valletta (pop 9,200)

YUGOSLAVIA

Until 1991, Yugoslavia (area 98,766 sq miles/255,804 sq km; pop 23,861,000; capital, Belgrade) was a federal republic. It consisted of six republics, each with its own parliament. In 1991-1992, four republics declared themselves independent. They are:

Croatia (cap Zagreb)

Slovania (cap Ljubljana)

Bosnia and Hercegovina (cap Sarajevo)

Macedonia (cap Skopje)

The other two republics declared that they would stay together and be known jointly as Yugoslavia. They are:

Montenegro (cap Titograd)

Serbia (cap Belgrade)

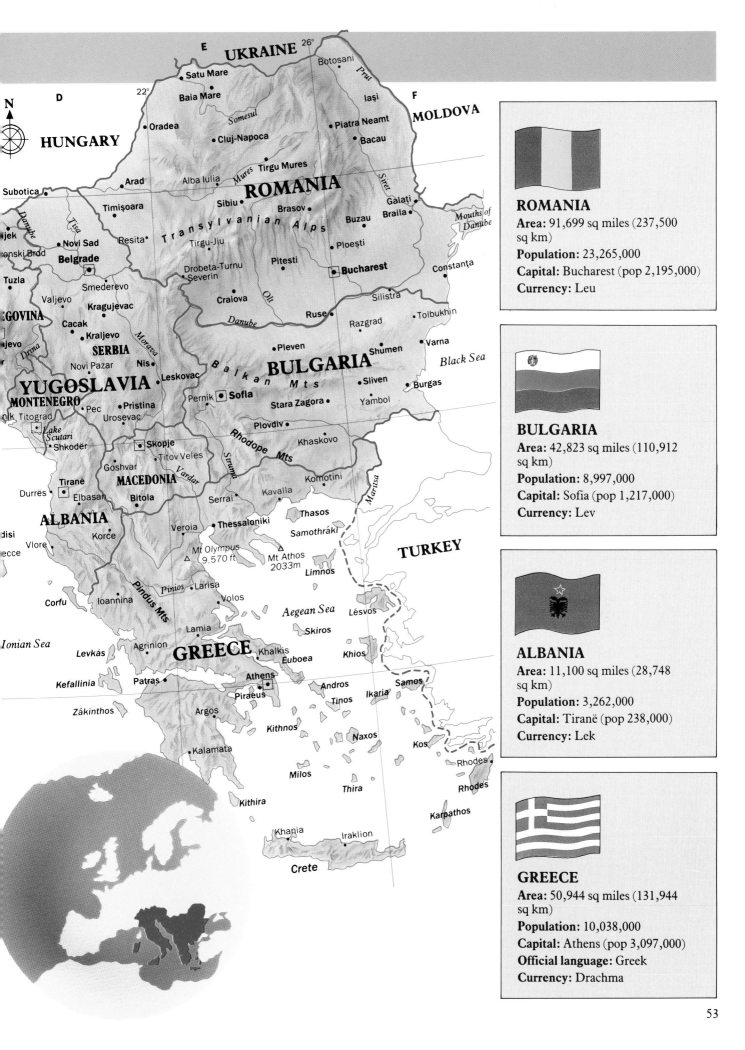

N

D E UKRAINE 26°

HUNGARY

22°

• Satu Mare

• Baia Mare

• Oradea

• Cluj-Napoca

• Botosani

Prut

• Iași F

• Piatra Neamt MOLDOVA

• Bacau

Somesul

Subotica • • Arad Alba Iulia Mures Tirgu Mures

Timișoara ROMANIA

• Sibiu • Brasov Siret • Galați

Transylvanian Alps • Buzau • Braila

jek Danube Tisa • Resita Tirgu-Jiu • Ploești Mouths of Danube

• Novi Sad Drobeta-Turnu • Pitesti □ Bucharest

onski Brod Belgrade □ • Severin • Constanța

Tuzla • Smederevo • Craiova Olt Danube • Silistra

Valjevo • Ruse • Razgrad • Tolbukhin

EGOVINA • Kragujevac

Cacak • Pleven Black Sea

• Kraljevo Moratva • Shumen • Varna

ajevo SERBIA Balkan Mts BULGARIA

Drina Novi Pazar • Nis • • Sliven • Burgas

YUGOSLAVIA • Leskovac Pernik □ Sofia • Sliven

MONTENEGRO • Pec • Pristina Stara Zagora • Yambol

nlk Titograd • Urosevac Plovdiv •

□ Lake • Shkodër □ Skopje Rhodope • Khaskovo

Scutari • Titov Veles Mts

Goshvar Struma • Komotini

Tiranë MACEDONIA Vardar

Durrës □ • Elbasan Bitola • Serrai • Kavalla Maritsa

ALBANIA • Thasos

disi Veroia • Thessaloniki Samothráki TURKEY

Vlore Korce

ecce Mt Olympus Mt Athos

△ 9,570 ft 2033m Limnos

Pindus Pinios Larisa

Corfu Mts • Ioannina • Volos Lésvos

Ionian Sea Aegean Sea

Levkás Agrinion Lamia Skiros Khios

GREECE Khalkis

Kefallinia Patras • Euboea Samos

Athens □ Andros Ikaria

Zákinthos Piraeus Tinos

Argos Kithnos Naxos Kos

• Kalamata Rhodes

Milos Thira Rhodes

Kithira Karpathos

Khania Iraklion

Crete

ROMANIA
Area: 91,699 sq miles (237,500 sq km)
Population: 23,265,000
Capital: Bucharest (pop 2,195,000)
Currency: Leu

BULGARIA
Area: 42,823 sq miles (110,912 sq km)
Population: 8,997,000
Capital: Sofia (pop 1,217,000)
Currency: Lev

ALBANIA
Area: 11,100 sq miles (28,748 sq km)
Population: 3,262,000
Capital: Tiranë (pop 238,000)
Currency: Lek

GREECE
Area: 50,944 sq miles (131,944 sq km)
Population: 10,038,000
Capital: Athens (pop 3,097,000)
Official language: Greek
Currency: Drachma

Russia and Its Neighbors

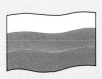

RUSSIAN FEDERATION (RUSSIA)

Area: 6,592,849 sq miles (17,075,400 sq km), the world's largest country

Highest point: Mount Elbrus 18,481 ft (5,633 m)

Population: 147,400,000

Capital: Moscow (pop 8,769,000)

Other cities:
St. Petersburg (4,456,000)
Nizhny Novgorod (1,438,000)
Novosibirsk (1,436,000)
Yekaterinburg (1,367,000)
Samara (1,257,000)

Official language: Russian

Religions: Christianity, Judaism, Islam

Main products: *Agriculture:* cotton, flax, potatoes, sugar, wheat, cattle, pigs, sheep; *Mining:* coal, copper, gold, iron ore, oil and natural gas; *Industry:* iron and steel, chemicals, machinery, paper, plastics

Currency: Rouble

Government: Federal republic

ESTONIA

Area: 17,413 sq miles (45,100 sq km)

Population: 1,573,000

Capital: Tallinn (pop 482,000)

LATVIA

Area: 24,904 sq miles (64,500 sq km)

Population: 2,680,000

Capital: Riga (pop 915,000)

LITHUANIA

Area: 25,174 sq miles (65,200 sq km)

Population: 3,690,000

Capital: Vilnius (pop 582,000)

BELARUS

Area: 80,155 sq miles (207,600 sq km)

Population: 10,200,000

Capital: Minsk (pop 1,589,000)

UKRAINE

Area: 233,090 sq miles (603,700 sq km)

Population: 51,707,000

Capital: Kiev (pop 2,587,000)

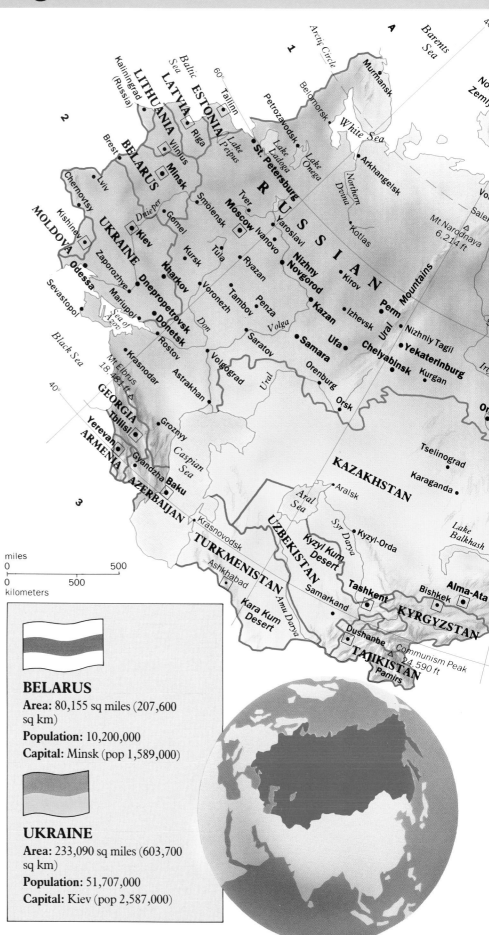

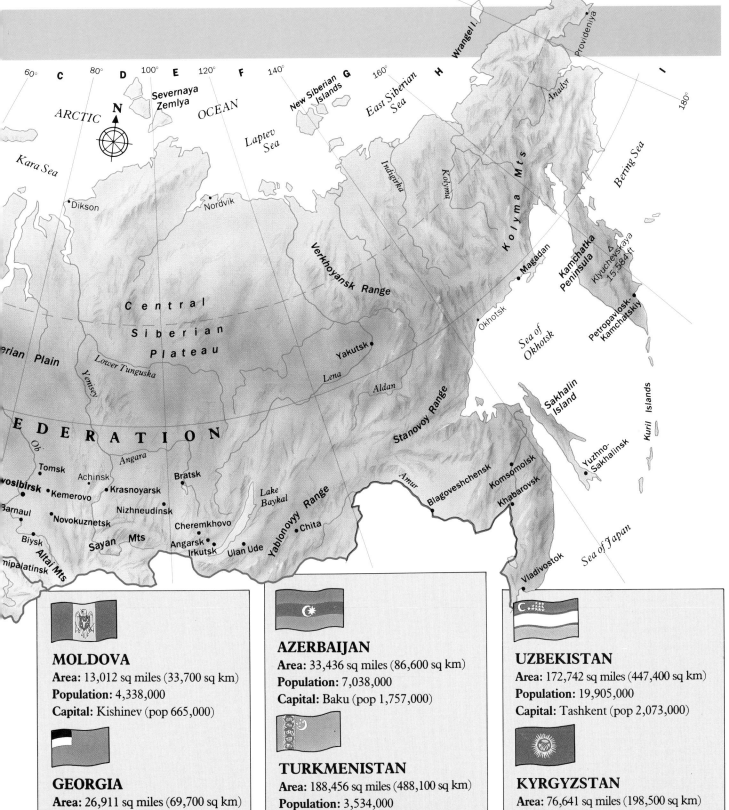

ARCTIC OCEAN

60° **C** 80° **D** 100° **E** 120° **F** 140° **G** 160° **H** 180° **I**

N

Kara Sea

Severnaya Zemlya

Laptev Sea

New Siberian Islands

East Siberian Sea

Wrangel I.

Providenya

Anadyr

Bering Sea

• Dikson

• Nordvik

Verkhoyansk Range

Kolyma Mts

Kolyma

Indigirka

Magadan

Kamchatka Peninsula

Klyucheyskaya △ 15,584 ft

Central Siberian Plateau

Lower Tunguska

Yenisey

Lena

Yakutsk •

Aldan

Okhotsk •

Sea of Okhotsk

Petropavlosk-Kamchatskiy •

erian Plain

F E D E R A T I O N

Ob

Angara

Stanovoy Range

Sakhalin Island

Kuril Islands

• Tomsk

Achinsk •

Krasnoyarsk •

• Bratsk

Lake Baykal

Amur

Blagoveshchensk •

Komsomolsk •

Khabarovsk •

Yuzhno-Sakhalinsk •

vosibirsk • Kemerovo •

Nizhneudinsk •

Cheremkhovo •

Yablonovyy Range

• Chita

Barnaul •

Novokuznetsk •

Angarsk •

Biysk •

Sayan Mts

Irkutsk • Ulan Ude

nipalatinsk •

Altai Mts

Sea of Japan

Vladivostok •

MOLDOVA
Area: 13,012 sq miles (33,700 sq km)
Population: 4,338,000
Capital: Kishinev (pop 665,000)

GEORGIA
Area: 26,911 sq miles (69,700 sq km)
Population: 5,443,000
Capital: Tbilisi (pop 1,260,000)

ARMENIA
Area: 11,506 sq miles (29,800 sq km)
Population: 3,288,000
Capital: Yerevan (pop 1,199,000)

AZERBAIJAN
Area: 33,436 sq miles (86,600 sq km)
Population: 7,038,000
Capital: Baku (pop 1,757,000)

TURKMENISTAN
Area: 188,456 sq miles (488,100 sq km)
Population: 3,534,000
Capital: Ashkhabad (pop 398,000)

KAZAKHSTAN
Area: 1,049,156 sq miles (2,717,300 sq km)
Population: 16,536,000
Capital: Alma-Ata (pop 1,128,000)

UZBEKISTAN
Area: 172,742 sq miles (447,400 sq km)
Population: 19,905,000
Capital: Tashkent (pop 2,073,000)

KYRGYZSTAN
Area: 76,641 sq miles (198,500 sq km)
Population: 4,290,000
Capital: Bishkek (pop 616,000)

TAJIKISTAN
Area: 55,251 sq miles (143,100 sq km)
Population: 5,109,000
Capital: Dushanbe (pop 595,000)

Asia

Asia is the largest continent. It contains China, Japan, India, and the major part of the Russian Federation, along with several other countries that were formerly part of the Soviet Union. These countries include Armenia, Azerbaijan, and Georgia, which lie south of the Caucasus Mountains. The other countries are Kazakhstan, Kyrgyzstan, Tajikistan, Turkmenistan, and Uzbekistan. These countries lie between the Caspian Sea in the west and China in the east.

China's Chang Jiang (formerly called the Yangtze Kiang) is the longest river. Mount Everest, on Nepal's border with China, is Asia's highest peak.

Asia has more than 3 billion people. It includes the world's two most populous countries, China, with more than 1 billion people, and India, with about 850 million people.

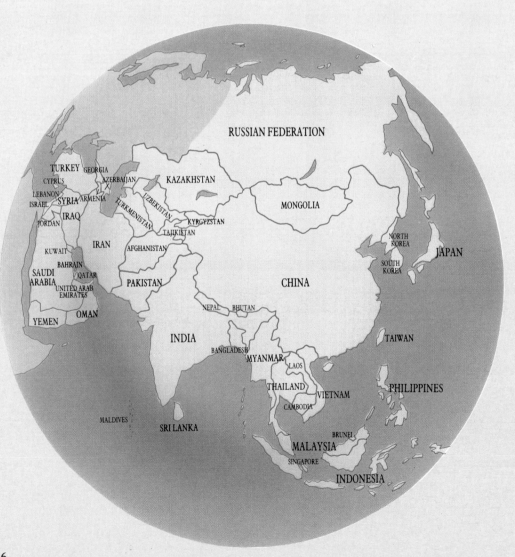

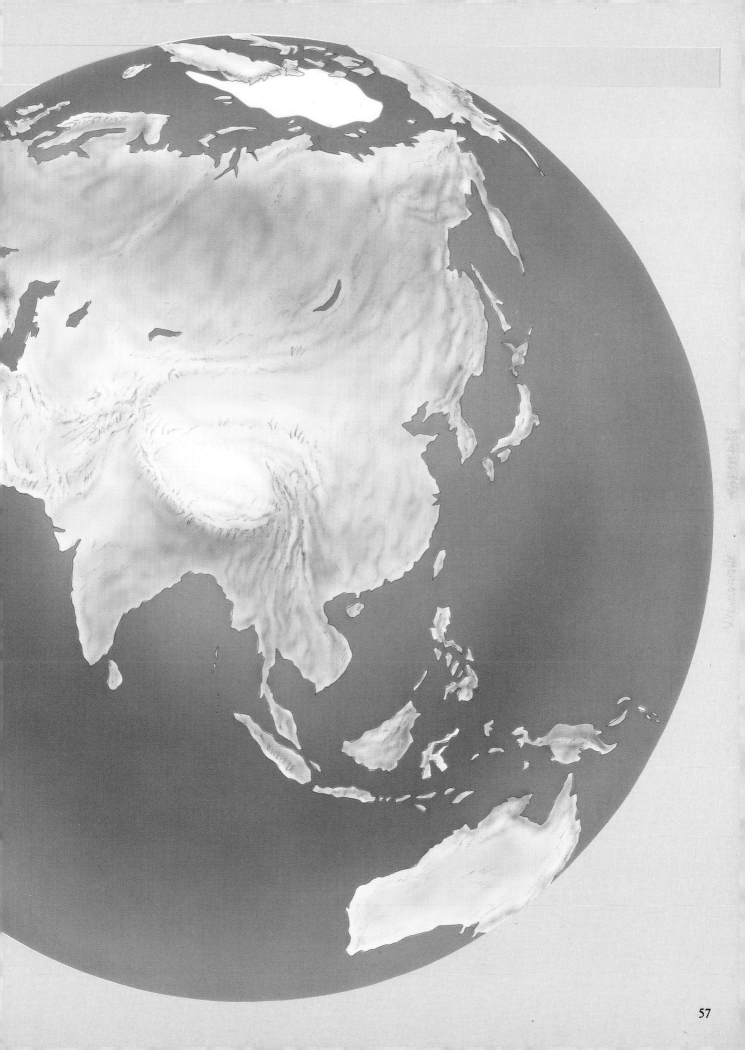

Near East

CYPRUS

Area: 3,572 sq miles (9,251 sq km)
Population: 568,000
Capital and largest city: Nicosia
(pop 167,000)

ISRAEL

Area: 8,019 sq miles (20,770 sq km
Population: 4,666,000
Capital and largest city: Jerusalem
(pop 495,000)
Other large cities:
Tel Aviv-Yafo (318,000)
Haifa (223,000)
Holon (146,000)
Official languages: Hebrew, Arabic
Religions: Judaism (81.5%), Islam
(13.9%), Christianity (2.3%), other
including Druze (2.3%)
Currency: Shekel

TURKEY

Area: 301,382 sq miles (780,576 sq km)
Population: 56,941,000
Capital: Ankara (pop 2,553,000)
Other large cities:
Istanbul (6,748,000)
Izmir (1,763,000)
Adana (932,000)
Bursa (838,000)
Official language: Turkish
Religion: Islam (99.2%)
Currency: Turkish Lira

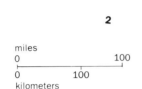

A | | | B

GREECE

1

Edirne 28°

Tekirdag **Istanbul** •Üsküdar

Sea of Marmara Izmit

•Adap

Gokceada I. Dardanelles

40° •Çanakkale

∴Troy •Bursa Sakarya

•Edremit •Balikesir Eskişehir

Aegean Sea •Bergama •Kütahy

Manisa

2 •Izmir Gediz •Uşak

miles
0 ————————— 100
0 ————— 100
kilometers

Aydin Menderes Lak
Egrid

•Denizli Isp

36° •An

•Finike

LEBANON

Area: 4,015 sq miles (10,400 sq km)
Population: 2,965,000
Capital and largest city: Beirut
(pop 1,500,000)
Currency: Lebanese Pound

3

JORDAN

Area: 37,738 sq miles (97,740 sq km)
Population: 3,169,000
Capital and largest city: Amman
(pop 936,000)
Currency: Jordanian Dinar

32°   C   36°   D   40°   E   44°   F

• Zonguldak   Samsun •   Black Sea   Rize •   GEORGIA

Çankiri •   *Kizil*   • Corum   *Kelkit*   Trabzon •   Kars •   ARMENIA

Ankara ⊡   Sivas •   Erzincan   Erzurum •   Mt Ararat △ 16,945 ft   IRAN

T U R K E Y   Elazig •   *Aras*   Lake Van   • Van

Lake Tuz   Kayseri •   Malatya •   Diyarbakir •   Batman •   K U R D I S T A N   *Tigris*

ake Beyşehir   • Konya   *Seyhan*   Maraş •   • Urfa   Nusaybin •

• Karaman   *Ceyhan*   • Osmaniye   Gaziantep •

Taurus   Mountains   Tarsus •   Adana •

Mersin •   • Iskenderun   • Aleppo   *Assad Reservoir*   *Euphrates*   *Khabur*   IRAQ

• Silifke   Antakya •   ∴ Ebla   Deir-ez-Zor •

Latakia •   S Y R I A

CYPRUS   Nicosia ⊡   • Hama   Mari •

• Famagusta   Krak des Chevaliers   Palmyra   ∴

• Larnaca   • Homs   ∴

Paphos   • Limassol   Tripoli •

Mediterranean Sea   **LEBANON**   *Anti-Lebanon Mts*

Beirut ⊡   Zahlé •

Sidon •   ☐ Damascus   *Syrian*

Tyre •   *Golan   Heights*   *Desert*

Haifa •   *Lake Tiberias*   Irbid •   • Busra

ISRAEL   *Jordan*

Ramat Gan •   Nablus •

Tel Aviv-Yafo •   *West Bank*   • Zarqa

Holon •   Jerusalem ☐   ⊡ Amman

Gaza Strip   Hebron •   *Dead Sea*

Beersheba •   **SAUDI ARABIA**

4   **JORDAN**

Negev Desert

EGYPT   Petra •

Ma'an •

Elat •   Aqaba •

SYRIA

Area: 71,498 sq miles (185,180 sq km)

Population: 12,116,000

Capital and largest city: Damascus (pop 1,361,000)

Other large cities: Aleppo (1,308,000)

Official language: Arabic

Currency: Syrian Pound

Arabian Peninsula and Gulf States

IRAQ
Area: 167,925 sq miles (434,924 sq km)
Population: 17,754,000
Capital and largest city: Baghdad (pop 5,438,000)
Other large cities: Basra (617,000)
Official language: Arabic
Currency: Iraqi Dinar

SAUDI ARABIA
Area: 830,000 sq miles (2,149,690 sq km)
Population: 14,131,000
Capital: Riyadh (pop 1,308,000)
Other large cities: Jiddah (1,500,000)
Official language: Arabic
Currency: Saudi Riyal

A   40°   B   45°   C   50°

N

TURKEY
Khvoy
Orumiyeh   • Tabriz   • Ardabil   *Caspian S.*
Kurdistan   Lake Urmia   • Rasht
1
Mosul   Zanjan   *Elburz*
• Irbil   Qazvin • Demavend
• Kirkuk   Qom   18,386 ft
35°   **Tehran**
SYRIA   *Euphrates*   *Tigris*   Bakhtaran Hamadan   • Qom
I R A Q   Borujerd   • Arak   Kasha
Ar Ramadi • • **Baghdad**   Khorramabad *Zagros* Esfa
2
Syrian Desert   Karbala • • Al Hillah   • Dezful *Mountains*
An Najaf •   • Al Amarah • Shushtar
JORDAN   An Nasiriyah   • Ahvaz
Ur   Basra Khorramshahr
30°   • Abadan
Al Jawf •   **KUWAIT**
KUWAIT   S
• Tabuk   A n   N a f u d   • Kuwait   Bushi
3   • Hafar
• Hail   *The Gul*
Buraydah •   Al Qatif • Damman
Al Wajh •   *H*   Dhahran • ▫ Al
e   **BAHRAIN** Mana
j
25°   *a* Al Hufuf •   **QAT**
z • Medina   ▫ **Riyadh**
Yanbu   Haradh •
Tropic of Cancer
4
Red Sea   **S   A   U   D   I**
Jiddah • • Mecca
• At Taif   **A   R   A   B   I   A**
20°   *R u b   a l   K h a l i*
Abha •
5   *H a d h r a m a u t*
• Jizan
Farasan Is.
△ ▫ Sana
15°   12,336 ft   **YEMEN**
Al Hudaydah •
Zabid •   Mukalla •
6
Mocha • • Taiz   Shuqra •
• Aden

60

55° E 60° F

TURKMENISTAN

• Gorgan

Neyshabur • Mashhad

Dasht-e Kavir

Dasht-e Lut

• Birjand

• Yazd

I R A N

• Kerman

Zahedan

• Bam

AFGHANISTAN

PAKISTAN

Bandar Abbas

Strait of Hormuz

Chah Bahar

Sharjah
Dubai
Dhabi
UNITED ARAB EMIRATES

Gulf of Oman

Al Khaburah

Muscat

△ 9,957 ft

OMAN

Al Masira

h u f a r

Salalah • Kuria Muria Is.

Arabian Sea

miles
0   200
0   200
kilometers

IRAN
Area: 636,296 sq miles (1,648,000 sq km)
Population: 56,293,000
Capital and largest city: Tehran (pop 6,043,000)
Other large cities: Mashhad (1,464,000) Esfahan (987,000)
Official language: Farsi (Persian)
Currency: Iranian Rial

KUWAIT
Area: 6,880 sq miles (17,818 sq km)
Population: 2,143,000
Capital: Kuwait (pop 44,000)
Currency: Kuwaiti Dinar

YEMEN
Area: 203,850 sq miles (527,968 sq km)
Population: 11,546,000
Capital and largest city: Sana (pop 427,000)
Other large city: Aden (318,000)
Currency: Yemen Rial

BAHRAIN
Area: 240 sq miles (622 sq km)
Population: 503,000
Capital: Al Manamah (pop 151,000)

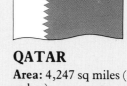

QATAR
Area: 4,247 sq miles (11,000 sq km)
Population: 444,000
Capital and largest city: Doha (pop 217,000)

UNITED ARAB EMIRATES
Area: 32,278 sq miles (83,600 sq km)
Population: 1,903,000
Capital: Abu Dhabi (pop 537,000)

OMAN
Area: 82,030 sq miles (212,457 sq km)
Population: 1,468,000
Capital and largest city: Muscat (pop 85,000)
Religions: Islam (86%), Hinduism (13%)
Currency: Omani Rial

India and Southern Asia

AFGHANISTAN

Area: 250,000 sq miles (647,497 sq km)

Population: 15,592,000

Capital and largest city: Kabul (pop 1,424,000)

Religion: Islam (99%)

Currency: Afghani

INDIA

Area: 1,269,346 sq miles (3,287,590 sq km)

Highest point: Kanchenjunga, on border with Nepal, 28,208 ft (8,598 m)

Population: 853,373,000

Capital: New Delhi (pop 273,000)

Other large cities:
Calcutta (10,916,000)
Bombay (9,990,000)
Delhi (7,175,000)
Madras (3,795,000)
Ahmedabad (2,875,000)
Bangalore (2,651,000)

Official languages: Hindi, English

Religions: Hinduism (82.6%), Islam (11.4%), Christianity (2.4%), Sikhism (2%), other religions (1.6%)

Economy: *Agriculture:* rice and other grains, pulses, cotton, sugar cane; *Fishing:* sea fishing; *Mining:* coal, iron ore, manganese; *Industry:* textiles, food products, machinery, steel, transportation equipment

Currency: Indian Rupee

Government: Federal republic

PAKISTAN

Area: 307,374 sq miles (796,095 sq km)

Population: 122,666,000

Capital: Islamabad (pop 204,000)

Other large cities:
Karachi (5,208,000)
Lahore (2,953,000)

Official language: Urdu

Religion: Islam (96.7%)

Main products: Rice, cotton, textiles

Currency: Pakistan Rupee

NEPAL

Area: 54,362 sq miles (140,797 sq km)

Highest point: Mount Everest, on the border with China, 29,028 ft (8,848 m)

Population: 18,910,000

Capital and largest city: Katmandu (pop 422,000)

Official language: Nepali

Currency: Nepali Rupee

The ownership of this area, is disputed.

C 75°

Chitral
Nanga Parbat △ 26,660 ft
Pass
Mardan
Islamabad
Rawalpindi
Gujranwala
godha
alabad Lahore
Amritsar
Jullundur
Ludhiana
Patiala
Chandigarh
Saharanpur
Dehra Dun
Meerut
Delhi
New Delhi
Bikaner
Alwar
Moradabad
Bareilly
Aligarh
Ajmer Jaipur
Agra
pur
Gwalior
Kanpur
Kota
Jhansi
Allahabad
adabad
Bhopal
Sagar
Vadodara
Ujjain
Narmada
Jabalpur
Indore
Burhanpur
Nagpur
Amravati
Bilaspur
INDIA
Raipur
Godavari
Aurangabad
Berhampur
bay
Pune
Sholapur
Warangal
Deccan
Hyderabad
hapur
Krishna
Vishakhapatnam
Belgaum
Plateau
Rajahmundry
Hubli
Vijayawada
Guntur
Davangere
alore
Bangalore
Madras
Mysore
Calicut
Salem
Coimbatore
Tiruchirappalli
Cochin
Madurai
Jaffna
Tirunelveli
Trivandrum
Gulf of Mannar
Trincomalee
AN
SRI LANKA
Colombo
Kandy
Galle

Gilgit
Karakoram Range
K2
△ 28,251 ft
Srinagar
Leh
D 80°

N

95°

HIMALAYA

Silgarhi
NEPAL
Annapurna △ 26,503 ft
Pokhara
Katmandu
E 85° F CHINA G 90°
Everest 29,028 ft △
Kanchenjunga 28,208 ft △
Thimphu
BHUTAN
Brahmaputra
Gauhati
Lucknow
Faizabad
Gorakhpur
Patna
Saidpur
Varanasi
Bhagalpur
Imphal
Gaya
BANGLADESH
Dhanbad
Rajshahi
Asansol
Dhaka
Narayanganj
Ranchi
Khulna
MYANMAR
Howrah
Jamshedpur
Calcutta
Chittagong
Cuttack

Bay of Bengal

miles
0   200
0   200
kilometers

Eastern Ghats

Eastern Ghats

BHUTAN
Area: 18,147 sq miles (47,000 sq km)
Population: 1,442,000
Capital: Thimphu (pop 20,000)

SRI LANKA
Area: 25,332 sq miles (65,610 sq km)
Population: 17,103,000
Capital and largest city: Colombo (pop 1,200,000)
Official languages: Sinhalese, Tamil
Currency: Sri Lankan Rupee

BANGLADESH
Area: 55,598 sq miles (143,998 sq km)
Population: 113,005,000
Capital and largest city: Dhaka (pop 5,300,000)
Other large city: Chittagong (2,030,000)
Official language: Bengali
Religions: Islam (86.6%), Hinduism (12.1%)
Currency: Taka

China, Japan, and the Far East

CHINA

Area: 3,705,408 sq miles (9,596,961 sq km)

Highest point: Mount Everest, on the border with Nepal, 29,028 ft (8,848 m)

Longest river: Chang Jiang (formerly Yangtze Kiang) 3,436 miles (5,530km)

Population: 1,133,683,000

Capital: Beijing (pop 6,800,000)

Other large cities:
Shanghai (7,330,000)
Tianjin (5,620,000)
Shenyang (4,440,000)
Wuhan (3,640,000)

Official language: Mandarin Chinese

Religions: Confucianism, Buddhism, Taoism, Islam

Economy: *Agriculture:* rice, wheat, oilseed, cotton; *Fishing:* fresh and sea fishing; *Mining:* coal, iron, oil; *Industry:* iron and steel, machinery, textiles

Currency: Yuan

Government: People's Republic

MONGOLIA

Area: 604,250 sq miles (1,565,000 sq km)

Population: 2,116,000

Capital and largest city: Ulan Bator (pop 548,000)

Official language: Mongolian

Religion: No figures

Currency: Tugrik

USSIA

120°

Lesser Hinggan Range

Greater Hinggan Range

E

132°

F

144°

•Qiqihar

Amur

•Harbin

Jixi

Baicheng

Manchurian
Plain

•Mudanjiang

Changchun •Jilin

Siping

Asahikawa

Shenyang

Fuxin

•Benxi

Sapporo

Hokkaido

•Anshan

Jinzhou

Hamhung

Hakodate

Aomori

•Morioka

Chongjin

Sea of
Japan

Akita

Sendai

Beijing

Tangshan

Pyongyang

NORTH KOREA

Niigata

JAPAN

Wonsan

Honshu

Tokyo

Tianjin •

Bo Hai
Sea

Dalian

Sinuiju

Nampo

Seoul

Kanazawa

Kawasaki

Chiba

Yokohama

Shijiazhuang

Yantai

Inchon

SOUTH KOREA

Kyoto

Nagoya

•uan

•Xingtai

Zibo

Weifang

Taejon

Taegu

Kobe

Osaka

Sakai

Mt Fuji
12,388 ft

•Qingdao

Ulsan

Okayama

an•

Jinan

Pusan

Matsuyama

•Kaifeng

Lianyungang

Yellow Sea

Kwangju

Hiroshima

Shikoku

g•

Xuzhou

Cheju

Kitakyushu

nyang

Huainan

Fukuoka

Kumamoto

Nanjing

Nantong

Nagasaki

Kyushu

Hefei

•Wuxi

Shanghai

Kagoshima

PACIFIC
OCEAN

Wuhan

Suzhou

Wuhu

East
China Sea

Hangzhou

ngshi

•Anqing

•Ningbo

•Jingdezhen

Nanchang

Wenzhou

Ryukyu Islands

•Naha

ngsha

ngyang

Fuzhou

Chilung

Taipei

Tropic of Cancer

•Shaoguan

Xiamen

Taichung

gzhou

Shantou

Tainan

TAIWAN

Gaoxlong

AO
HONG
KONG (U.K.)

t.)

South China Sea

miles
0   500

0   500
kilometers

JAPAN

Area: 145,800 sq miles (377,708 sq km)

Highest point: Mount Fuji 12,388 ft (3,776 m)

Population: 123,692,000

Capital: Tokyo (pop 8,278,000)

Other large cities: Yokohama (3,191,000) Osaka (2,635,000)

Official language: Japanese

Religions: Shintoism (39.5%), Buddhism (38.3%)

Main products: Manufactures, including machinery, vehicles, electronic goods, instruments

Currency: Yen

Government: Monarchy

NORTH KOREA

Area: 46,540 sq miles (120,538 sq km)

Population: 22,937,000

Capital and largest city: Pyongyang (pop 2,000,000)

SOUTH KOREA

Area: 38,025 sq miles (98,484 sq km)

Population: 42,793,000

Capital and largest city: Seoul (pop 10,726,000)

TAIWAN

Area: 13,900 sq miles (36,000 sq km)

Population: 20,221,000

Capital and largest city: Taipei (pop 2,702,000)

HONG KONG

Area: 403 sq miles (1,045 sq km)

Population: 5,841,000

Capital: Victoria

MACAO

Area: 6 sq miles (16 sq km)

Population: 461,000

Capital: Macao

Southeastern Asia

THAILAND
Area: 198,457 sq miles (514,000 sq km)
Population: 56,217,000
Capital and largest city: Bangkok (pop 5,717,000)
Official language: Thai
Currency: Baht

MALAYSIA
Area: 127,317 sq miles (329,749 sq km)
Population: 17,886,000
Capital and largest city: Kuala Lumpur (pop 1,103,000)
Official language: Malay
Currency: Ringgit

SINGAPORE
Area: 224 sq miles (581 sq km)
Population: 2,718,000
Capital and largest city: Singapore (pop 2,685,000)
Official languages: Chinese, Malay, Tamil, English
Currency: Singapore Dollar

MYANMAR (Burma)
Area: 261,218 sq miles (676,552 sq km)
Population: 41,675,000
Capital and largest city: Yangon (formerly Rangoon, pop 2,513,000)
Official language: Burmese
Currency: Kyat

VIETNAM
Area: 127,242 sq miles (329,556 sq km)
Population: 66,128,000
Capital city: Hanoi (pop 3,100,000)
Currency: Dong

LAOS
Area: 91,429 sq miles (236,800 sq km)
Population: 4,024,000
Capital and largest city: Vientiane (pop 377,000)

BRUNEI
Area: 2,226 sq miles (5,765 sq km)
Population: 259,000
Capital and largest city: Bandar Seri Begawan (pop 52,000)

PHILIPPINES
Area: 115,831 sq miles (300,000 sq km)
Population: 61,480,000
Capital and largest city: Manila (pop 1,876,000)
Currency: Philippine Peso

CAMBODIA
Area: 69,898 sq miles (181,035 sq km)
Population: 8,592,000
Capital and largest city: Phnom Penh (pop 564,000)
Currency: Riel

INDONESIA
Area: 735,358 sq miles (1,904,569 sq km)
Population: 180,763,000
Capital and largest city: Jakarta (pop 8,800,000)
Currency: Rupiah

.0°

C   120°   D

South China Sea

Aparri

Luzon

Baguio

San Carlos

Caloocan

Manila

Batangas   Lucena

Mindoro

anh

PHILIPPINES

Mayon Volcano 7,943 ft   Samar   130°   E

Panay
Iloilo   Cadiz   Leyte
Bacolod   Cebu

Palawan

Negros   Bohol

Sulu Sea   Butuan
Iligan   Cagayan de Oro
Zamboanga   Mindanao
Basilan   Mt Apo   Davao
9,692 ft   General Santos

PACIFIC OCEAN

dar Seri Begawan
BRUNEI   Sabah
I A   Tawau   Celebes Sea   Talaud Is.

Sarawak   Sangihe Is.

ng

Manado   140°   F

ntang   Borneo   Halmahera
Waigeo   Manokwari

Samarinda   Sulawesi (Celebes)   Sarmi

Palu   Obi   Misool

Balikpapan   Sula Is.   Ceram Sea   New Guinea

alimantan   Ceram   Fakfak   Maoke   Range

E S I A   Ambon   Puncak Jaya   Irian
Banjarmasin   Majene   Buru   16,503 ft   Jaya   PAPUA NEW GUINEA
Kendari

Java Sea   Ujung Pandang   Banda Sea   Aru Is.

arang   Flores Sea
Surabaya   Wetar
akarta   Malang   Bali
karta   Lombok   Sumbawa   Flores   Dili   Tanimbar Is.   Merauke
Sumba   Timor

67

Africa

Africa is the world's second largest continent. Much of the land is wilderness. Areas with few people include the Sahara in North Africa, the world's biggest desert, and the Kalahari and Namib deserts in southern Africa. Africa has dense forests around the equator, together with huge grasslands, the home of many wild animals.

The continent's rivers include the world's longest, the Nile. The highest mountain is Kilimanjaro, an old volcano in Tanzania.

Africa contains 52 independent countries, with a total population of nearly 700 million. A few countries are rich in minerals and some have industries, but more than half of the people of Africa are poor farmers.

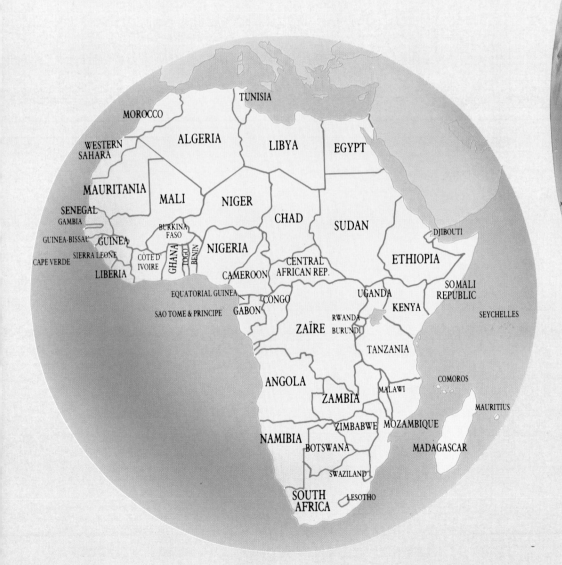

North Africa

ALGERIA
Area: 919,595 sq miles (2,381,741 sq km)
Population: 25,337,000
Capital: Algiers (pop 1,507,000)

TUNISIA
Area: 63,170 sq miles (163,610 sq km)
Population: 8,182,000
Capital: Tunis (pop 597,000)

MAURITANIA
Area: 397,956 sq miles (1,030,700 sq km)
Population: 1,999,000
Capital: Nouakchott (pop 600,000)

MOROCCO
Area: 172,414 sq miles (446,550 sq km)
Population: 25,113,000
Capital: Rabat (pop 519,000)

WESTERN SAHARA
(occupied by Morocco)
Area: 102,703 sq miles (266,000 sq km)
Population: 250,000

MALI
Area: 478,767 sq miles (1,240,000 sq km)
Population: 8,151,000
Capital: Bamako (pop 646,000)

NIGER
Area: 489,191 sq miles (1,267,000 sq km)
Population: 7,779,000
Capital: Niamey (pop 398,000)

N

LIBYA
Area: 679,362 sq miles (1,759,000 sq km)
Population: 4,206,000
Capital: Tripoli (pop 591,000)

CHAD
Area: 495,755 sq miles (1,284,000 sq km)
Population: 5,678,000
Capital: N'Djamena (pop 500,000)

EGYPT
Area: 386,662 sq miles (1,001,449 sq km)
Population: 53,170,000
Capital: Cairo (pop 6,053,000)

ETHIOPIA
Area: 471,778 sq miles (1,221,900 sq km)
Population: 50,341,000
Capital: Addis Ababa (pop 1,495,000)

DJIBOUTI
Area: 8,494 sq miles (22,000 sq km)
Population: 530,000
Capital: Djibouti (pop 220,000)

SOMALI REPUBLIC
Area: 246,201 sq miles (637,657 sq km)
Population: 7,555,000
Capital: Mogadishu (pop 500,000)

SUDAN
Area: 967,500 sq miles (2,505,813 sq km)
Population: 28,311,000
Capital: Khartoum (pop 476,000)

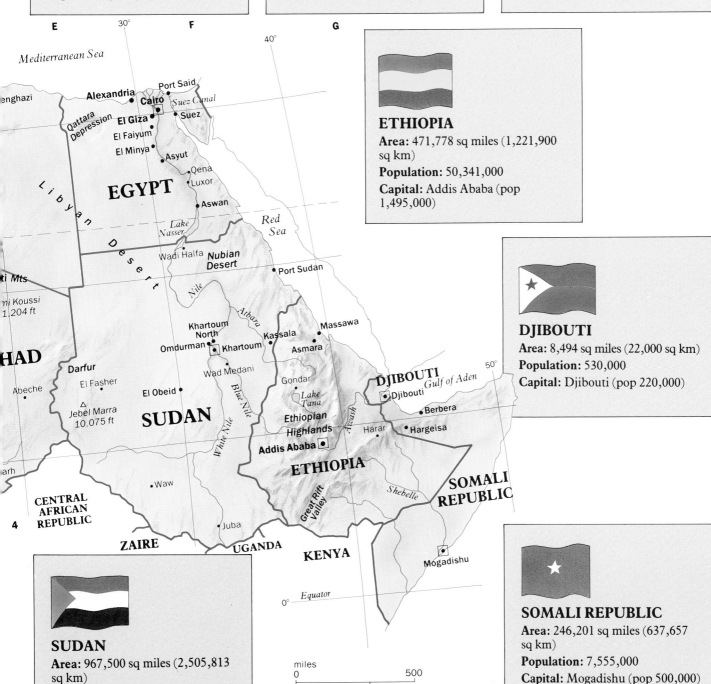

E 30° F 40° G

Mediterranean Sea

Benghazi
Alexandria
Port Said
Cairo
Suez Canal
Qattara
Depression
El Giza
Suez
El Faiyum
El Minya
Asyut
Libyan Desert
Qena
Luxor
EGYPT
Aswan
Lake Nasser
Red Sea
Wadi Halfa
Nubian Desert
Port Sudan
ti Mts
mi Koussi
1,204 ft
Nile
Atbara
Massawa
Khartoum North
Kassala
Asmara
Omdurman
Khartoum
HAD
Darfur
El Fasher
Wad Medani
Gondar
DJIBOUTI
Gulf of Aden
Abeche
El Obeid
Lake Tana
Djibouti
50°
△ Jebel Marra
10,075 ft
SUDAN
Blue Nile
Ethiopian
Highlands
Berbera
Harar
Hargeisa
Addis Ababa
White Nile
SOMALI
REPUBLIC
arh
ETHIOPIA
Shebelle
Waw
Great Rift Valley
CENTRAL
AFRICAN
REPUBLIC
4
Juba
ZAIRE
UGANDA
KENYA
Mogadishu
0° Equator

miles
0   500
0   500
kilometers

West Africa

Cape Verde Islands

Santa Antão

Sal I.

Boa Vista I.

Sào Tiago I.

Brava • Praia

CAPE VERDE
Area: 1,557 sq miles (4,033 sq km)
Population: 339,000
Capital: Praia (pop 55,000)

GAMBIA
Area: 4,361 sq miles (11,295 sq km)
Population: 860,000
Capital: Banjul (pop 44,000)

GUINEA-BISSAU
Area: 13,948 sq miles (36,125 sq km)
Population: 973,000
Capital: Bissau (pop 125,000)

GUINEA
Area: 94,926 sq miles (245,857 sq km)
Population: 6,876,000
Capital: Conakry (pop 705,000)

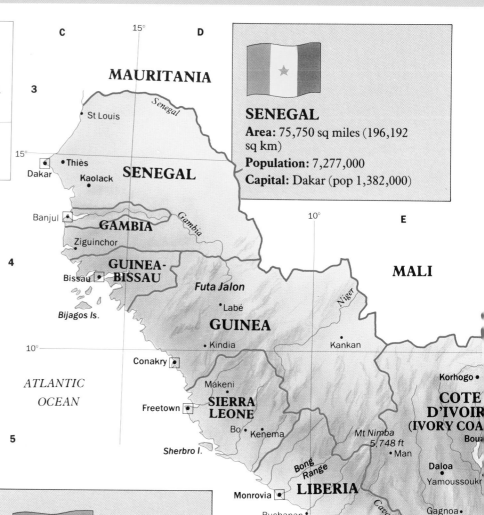

MAURITANIA

St Louis

Senegal

Dakar • Thiès

SENEGAL

Kaolack

Banjul

GAMBIA

Gambia

Ziguinchor

GUINEA-BISSAU

Bissau

Bijagos Is.

Futa Jalon

• Labé

GUINEA

• Kindia

Niger

Kankan

MALI

Conakry

Mákeni

SIERRA LEONE

Freetown

Bo •

Kenema

Sherbro I.

Mt Nimba 5,748 ft

• Man

Korhogo •

COTE D'IVOIRE (IVORY COAST)

Boua

Daloa •

Yamoussoukr

Bong Range

LIBERIA

Monrovia

Buchanan

Cavally

Sassandra

Gagnoa

ATLANTIC OCEAN

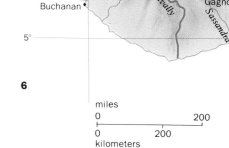

SENEGAL
Area: 75,750 sq miles (196,192 sq km)
Population: 7,277,000
Capital: Dakar (pop 1,382,000)

SIERRA LEONE
Area: 27,699 sq miles (71,740 sq km)
Population: 4,151,000
Capital: Freetown (pop 470,000)

LIBERIA
Area: 43,000 sq miles (111,369 sq km)
Population: 2,595,000
Capital: Monrovia (pop 421,000)

miles
0   200
0   200
kilometers

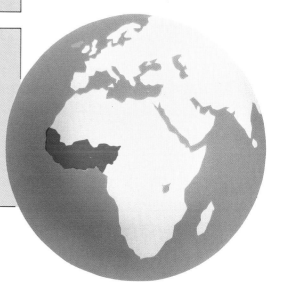

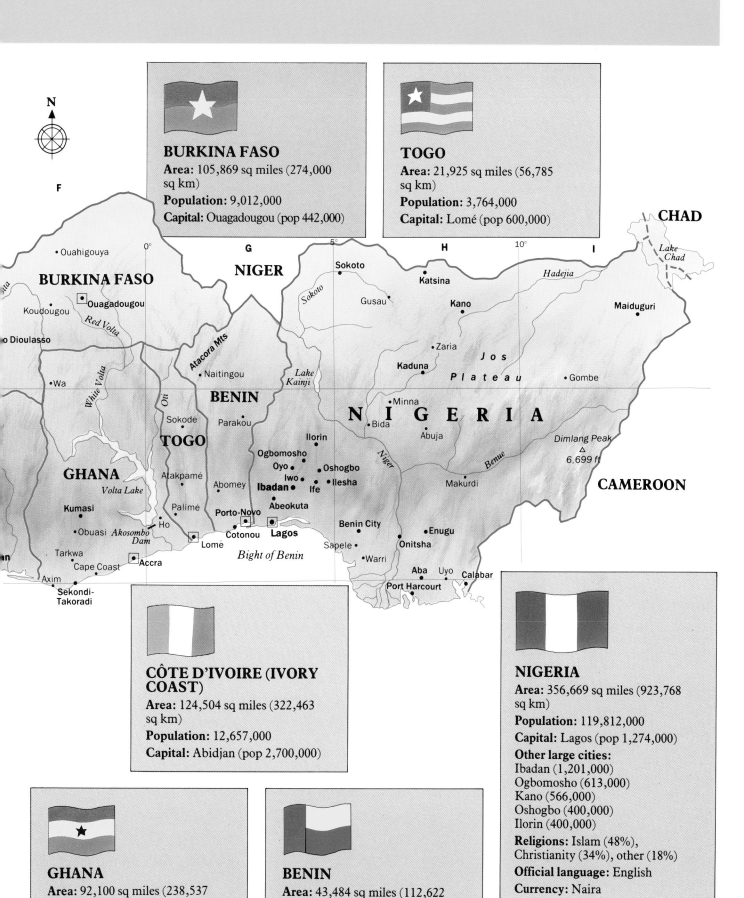

BURKINA FASO
Area: 105,869 sq miles (274,000 sq km)

Population: 9,012,000

Capital: Ouagadougou (pop 442,000)

TOGO
Area: 21,925 sq miles (56,785 sq km)

Population: 3,764,000

Capital: Lomé (pop 600,000)

CÔTE D'IVOIRE (IVORY COAST)
Area: 124,504 sq miles (322,463 sq km)

Population: 12,657,000

Capital: Abidjan (pop 2,700,000)

NIGERIA
Area: 356,669 sq miles (923,768 sq km)

Population: 119,812,000

Capital: Lagos (pop 1,274,000)

Other large cities:
Ibadan (1,201,000)
Ogbomosho (613,000)
Kano (566,000)
Oshogbo (400,000)
Ilorin (400,000)

Religions: Islam (48%), Christianity (34%), other (18%)

Official language: English

Currency: Naira

GHANA
Area: 92,100 sq miles (238,537 sq km)

Population: 15,020,000

Capital: Accra (pop 949,000)

BENIN
Area: 43,484 sq miles (112,622 sq km)

Population: 4,741,000

Capital: Porto-Novo (pop 208,000)

Central Africa

SÃO TOMÉ AND PRINCIPE
Area: 372 sq miles (964 sq km)
Population: 121,000
Capital: São Tomé (pop 35,000)

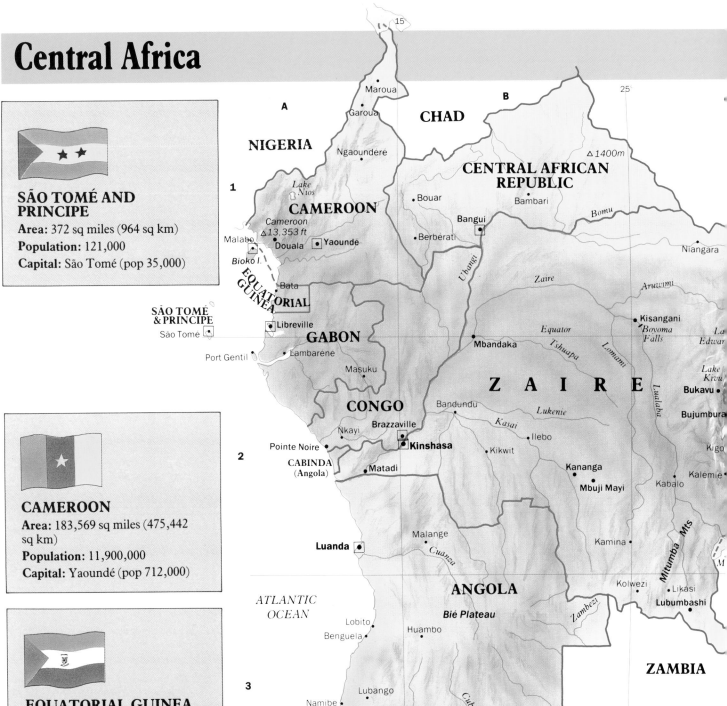

NIGERIA

CHAD

Maroua

Garoua

A

B

Ngaoundéré

CENTRAL AFRICAN
REPUBLIC

△1400m

Bouar

Bambari

Lake
Nios

CAMEROON

1

Bangui

Bomu

Berbérati

Niangara

Cameroon
△13.353 ft

Malabo

Douala

Yaoundé

Ubangi

Zaire

Aruwimi

Bioko I.

Bata

EQUATORIAL
GUINEA

Kisangani
Boyoma
Falls

La
Edwar

Libreville

Equator

Tshuapa

Lomami

SÃO TOMÉ
& PRINCIPE

São Tomé

GABON

Mbandaka

Z A I R E

Lake
Kivu

Port Gentil

Lambaréne

Masuku

Bukavu

Lualaba

Bujumbura

CONGO

Bandundu

Lukenie

Nkayi

Brazzaville

Kasai

Ilebo

Kigo

Pointe Noire

Kinshasa

Kikwit

Kananga

Kalemie

2

CABINDA
(Angola)

Matadi

Mbuji Mayi

Kabalo

Malange

Kamina

Mitumba Mts

Luanda

Cuanza

M

ATLANTIC
OCEAN

ANGOLA

Kolwezi

Likasi

Bié Plateau

Lubumbashi

Lobito

Huambo

Zambezi

ZAMBIA

Benguela

3

Namibe

Lubango

Cubango

Cunene

NAMIBIA

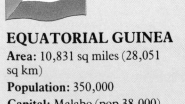

CAMEROON
Area: 183,569 sq miles (475,442 sq km)
Population: 11,900,000
Capital: Yaoundé (pop 712,000)

EQUATORIAL GUINEA
Area: 10,831 sq miles (28,051 sq km)
Population: 350,000
Capital: Malabo (pop 38,000)

GABON
Area: 103,347 sq miles (267,667 sq km)
Population: 1,171,000
Capital: Libreville (pop 352,000)

CONGO
Area: 132,047 sq miles (342,000 sq km)
Population: 2,326,000
Capital: Brazzaville (pop 596,000)

ANGOLA
Area: 481,354 sq miles (1,246,700 sq km)
Population: 10,002,000
Capital: Luanda (pop 1,134,000)

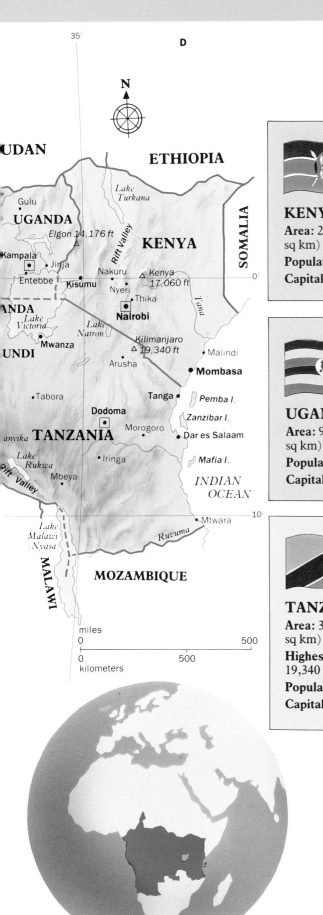

SUDAN

ETHIOPIA

Lake Turkana

Gulu

UGANDA

Elgon 14,176 ft △

Kampala □

Jinja

Entebbe

Kisumu

UANDA

Lake Victoria

RUNDI

Mwanza

Nakuru

KENYA

Nyeri

Kenya 17,060 ft △

Thika

Nairobi ■

Rift Valley

SOMALIA

Tana

0°

Kilimanjaro △ 19,340 ft

Malindi

Arusha

Mombasa

Tabora

Tanga

Pemba I.

Dodoma □

Zanzibar I.

Morogoro

Dar es Salaam

anyika

TANZANIA

Mafia I.

Lake Rukwa

Iringa

INDIAN OCEAN

Rift Valley

Mbeya

10°

Mtwara

Lake Malawi Nyasa

Ruvuma

MALAWI

MOZAMBIQUE

miles
0 ——————— 500
0 ——————— 500
kilometers

KENYA

Area: 224,961 sq miles (582,646 sq km)
Population: 24,872,000
Capital: Nairobi (pop 1,429,000)

UGANDA

Area: 91,134 sq miles (236,036 sq km)
Population: 16,928,000
Capital: Kampala (pop 459,000)

TANZANIA

Area: 364,900 sq miles (945,087 sq km)
Highest point: Mount Kilimanjaro 19,340 ft (5,895 m)
Population: 24,403,000
Capital: Dodoma (pop 204,000)

CENTRAL AFRICAN REPUBLIC

Area: 240,535 sq miles (622,984 sq km)
Population: 2,875,000
Capital: Bangui (pop 597,000)

ZAIRE

Area: 905,568 sq miles (2,345,409 sq km)
Population: 34,138,000
Capital: Kinshasa (pop 3,562,000)
Official language: French
Currency: Zaire

RWANDA

Area: 10,169 sq miles (26,338 sq km)
Population: 7,232,000
Capital: Kigali (pop 300,000)

BURUNDI

Area: 10,747 sq miles (27,834 sq km)
Population: 5,541,000
Capital: Bujumbura (pop 273,000)

Southern Africa

ZAMBIA
Area: 290,586 sq miles (752,614 sq km)
Population: 8,456,000
Capital: Lusaka (pop 870,000)

MALAWI
Area: 45,747 sq miles (118,484 sq km)
Population: 8,831,000
Capital: Lilongwe (pop 220,000)

NAMIBIA
Area: 318,261 sq miles (824,292 sq km)
Population: 1,302,000
Capital: Windhoek (pop 114,000)

B

30

C

40

ZAIRE

1

Lake Mweru

Lake Tanganyika

Kasama

Lake Bangweulu

TANZANIA

Ruvuma

A

20

Mufulira

Chingola

Kitwe • Ndola

Muchinga Mts

Lake Malawi (Nyasa)

Pem

ANGOLA

15

ZAMBIA

Kabwe

Luangwa

MALAWI

Lilongwe •

Lichinga

Shire

Nampula • Moçambiq

• Lusaka

Cabora Bassa Dam

Blantyre

Kafue

Zambezi

Okavango

Rundu

Caprivi Strip

Livingstone

• Kariba Dam

Lake Kariba

Tete •

MOZAMBIQUE

Quelimane

Namib

Etosha Pan

• Tsumeb

Victoria Falls

ZIMBABWE

Harare
•

Mutare •

Chimoio
•

2

Okavango Basin

Kwekwe •

NAMIBIA

Gweru •

• Masvingo

Mt Binga
7,972 ft

Beira •

Windhoek
•

Bulawayo
•

Walvis Bay
(S. Africa)

Desert

K a l a h a r i

Orapa •

Francistown •

Bobonong
•

Beitbridge •

Mozambique Channel

25

Lüderitz •

Keetmanshoop •

BOTSWANA

Serowe •

Mahalapye •

Limpopo

Pietersburg •

Tropic of Capricorn

Inhambane •

D e s e r t

Gaborone •

Xai Xai •

Upington •

Mafikeng •

Krugersdorp

Pretoria
•

INDIAN OCEAN

Orange

Kimberley •

Vaal

Johannesburg • • Springs
Germiston
Vereeniging

Potchefstroom •

• Maputo

Mbabane
•

SWAZILAND

ATLANTIC OCEAN

Bloemfontein •

Maseru
•

LESOTHO

• Kroonstad

Welkom •

• Newcastle

Ladysmith •

*Thabana Ntlenyana
11,424 ft*

• Pietermaritzburg

• Durban

3

SOUTH AFRICA

Beaufort West •

Drakensberg

Queenstown •

miles
0   500

Cape Town
•

Paarl •

Worcester •

Great Karroo

Little Karroo

Uitenhage •

• East London

0   500
kilometers

Mosselbaai •

• Port Elizabeth

Cape of Good Hope

MOZAMBIQUE
Area: 309,496 sq miles (801,590 sq km)

Population: 15,696,000

Capital: Maputo (pop 1,070,000)

COMOROS
Area: 838 sq miles (2,171 sq km)

Population: 463,000

Capital: Moroni (pop 22,000)

ZIMBABWE
Area: 150,804 sq miles (390,580 sq km)

Population: 9,369,000

Capital: Harare (pop 863,000)

SOUTH AFRICA
Area: 471,445 sq miles (1,221,037 sq km)

Population: 44,040,000

Capital: Pretoria (administrative, 850,000), Cape Town (legislative, 1,900,000), Bloemfontein (judicial, 103,000)

Other large cities: Durban (1,000,000) Johannesburg (1,700,000)

Religions: Christianity (78.1%), Hinduism (2.1%), Islam (1.4%), other (18.4%)

Official languages: Afrikaans, English

Currency: Rand

BOTSWANA
Area: 224,607 sq miles (581,730 sq km)

Population: 1,295,000

Capital: Gaborone (pop 111,000)

MADAGASCAR
Area: 226,658 sq miles (587,041 sq km)

Population: 11,980,000

Capital: Antananarivo (pop 802,000)

SWAZILAND
Area: 6,704 sq miles (17,363 sq km)

Population: 770,000

Capital: Mbabane (pop 38,000)

LESOTHO
Area: 11,720 sq miles (30,355 sq km)

Population: 1,760,000

Capital: Maseru (pop 109,000)

D   50'

N

COMOROS
ISLANDS

roni

Antsiranana

Maromokotro △
9,436 ft

Mahajanga

MADAGASCAR

Antananarivo ▪

Toamasina

Antsirabe •

Fianarantsoa •

oliara

Faradofay

Australia and Oceania

Australia is the only country that is also a continent. It is the smallest of the world's seven continents. Australia is part of a region called Oceania, which also includes New Zealand, Papua New Guinea, and many islands in the Pacific Ocean.

The longest river in Australia is the Murray. It flows throughout the year, unlike the slightly longer Darling River, parts of which dry up in winter. Papua New Guinea has the highest mountains in Oceania. New Zealand's highest peak is Mount Cook. Australia's is Mount Kosciusko.

Australia is a mainly dry continent, with only about 17 million people. Most Australians live in a few cities on the coast, including Sydney and Melbourne. The rest of Oceania has about 10 million people.

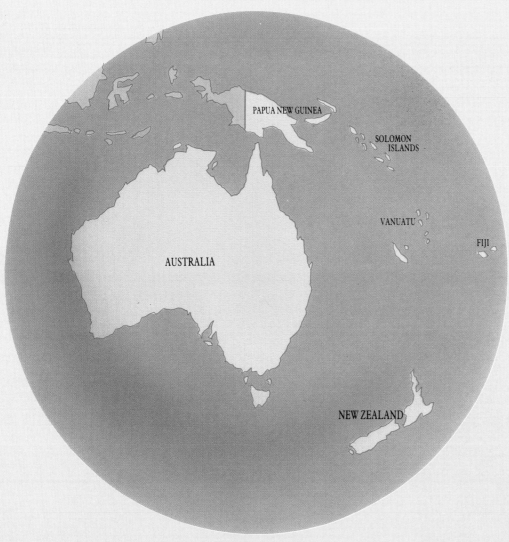

PAPUA NEW GUINEA

SOLOMON ISLANDS

VANUATU

FIJI

AUSTRALIA

NEW ZEALAND

Australia, New Zealand, and the Pacific Islands

130° C 140° D 150°

1

Wewak
Sepik
Bismarck Sea
New Ireland
Rabaul
Madang
New Britain
Mt Wilhelm
14,790 ft △
PAPUA NEW GUINEA
Lae
Bougair
Solomon .
Owen Stanley Range
Port Moresby ▫

Arafura Sea

10°
Torres Strait
Cape York
Melville I.

B *Timor Sea*
Darwin
Arnhem Land
Gulf of Carpentaria
Cape York Peninsula
Cooktown
Coral Sea
Cairns
Great

A INDIAN OCEAN
Wyndham
Kimberley Plateau
NORTHERN TERRITORY
Townsville
Barrier

2
Derby
Tennant Creek
Richmond
Mackay
Reef
Broome
Mount Isa
Great Dividing Range

Great Sandy Desert
A U S T R A L I A
QUEENSLAND
Rockhampton

20°
Dampier
Port Hedland
Macdonnell Range
Great Artesian Basin
Bundab
Carnarvon
Gibson Desert
Alice Springs
Simpson Desert
Maryboro
Ayers Rock
△ 2,844 ft
Musgrave Range
Lake Eyre
Toowoomba
Bris
WESTERN AUSTRALIA
SOUTH AUSTRALIA
Ipswich
C
3
Mount Magnet
Great Victoria Desert
Lism
Graft
Great Dividing Range

Lake Torrens
Bourke
Geraldton
Darling
Kalgoorlie
Nullarbor Plain
Lake Gairdner
Woomera
Broken Hill
NEW SOUTH WALES
Maitland
Norseman
Port Augusta
Newcastle
30°
Perth
Whyalla
Port Pirie
Sydney
Fremantle
Elizabeth
Wagga Wagga
Wollongong
Bunbury
Great Australian Bight
Adelaide
Canberra
AUSTRALIAN CAPITAL TERF
Albury
△Mt Kosciusko
VICTORIA
7,316 ft
Albany
Murray
Bendigo
Great
Kangaroo I.
Ballarat
4
Geelong **Melbourne**

King I.
Bass Strait **Flinders I.**

40°
△Mt Ossa 5,305 ft
TASMANIA
5
Hobart

miles
0   500
0   500
kilometers

80

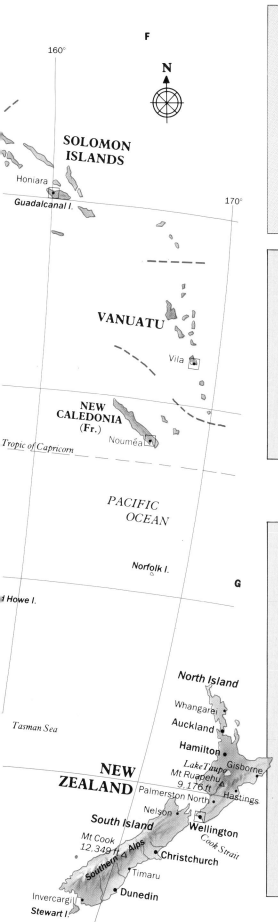

160°

F

N

SOLOMON
ISLANDS

Honiara

Guadalcanal I.

170°

VANUATU

Vila

NEW
CALEDONIA
(Fr.)

Nouméa

Tropic of Capricorn

PACIFIC
OCEAN

Norfolk I.

G

d Howe I.

Tasman Sea

North Island

Whangarei

Auckland

Hamilton

Lake Taupo   Gisborne
Mt Ruapehu
9,176 ft   Hastings

NEW   Palmerston North
ZEALAND

Nelson

South Island   Wellington
Cook Strait
Mt Cook
12,349 ft   Southern Alps   Christchurch

Timaru

Invercargill   Dunedin

Stewart I.

PAPUA NEW GUINEA

Area: 178,260 sq miles (461,691 sq km)

Highest point: Mount Wilhelm 14,790 ft (4,508 m)

Population: 3,671,000

Capital and largest city: Port Moresby (pop 152,000)

SOLOMON ISLANDS

Area: 10,983 sq miles (28,446 sq km)

Population: 319,000

Capital and largest city: Honiara (pop 30,000)

VANUATU

Area: 5,700 sq miles (14,763 sq km)

Population: 147,000

Capital: Vila (pop 19,000)

AUSTRALIA

Area: 2,967,909 sq miles (7,686,848 sq km)

Highest point: Mount Kosciusko 7,316 ft (2,230 m)

Population: 17,073,000

Capital: Canberra (pop 297,000)

Other large cities: Sydney (3,596,000), Melbourne (3,002,000), Brisbane (1,240,000)

Official language: English

Religion: Christianity

Economy: *Agriculture:* wool, meat, wheat, fruit, sugar; *Mining:* bauxite, coal, iron ore, copper, oil and natural gas, uranium; *Industry:* machinery and transportation equipment, processed foods, chemicals, iron and steel, paper, textiles

Currency: Australian Dollar

Government: Constitutional Monarchy

NEW ZEALAND

Area: 103,736 sq miles (268,676 sq km)

Population: 3,389,000

Capital: Wellington (pop 326,000)

Other large cities: Auckland (953,000), Christchurch (303,000)

Official language: English

Religion: Christianity

Economy: *Agriculture:* wool, meat, dairy products; *Mining:* natural gas, iron ore, coal; *Industry:* processed foods, wood and paper, textiles, machinery

Currency: New Zealand Dollar

Government: Constitutional Monarchy

NEW CALEDONIA (FRANCE)

Area: 7,358 sq miles (19,058 sq km)

Population: 168,000

Capital: Nouméa (pop 65,000)

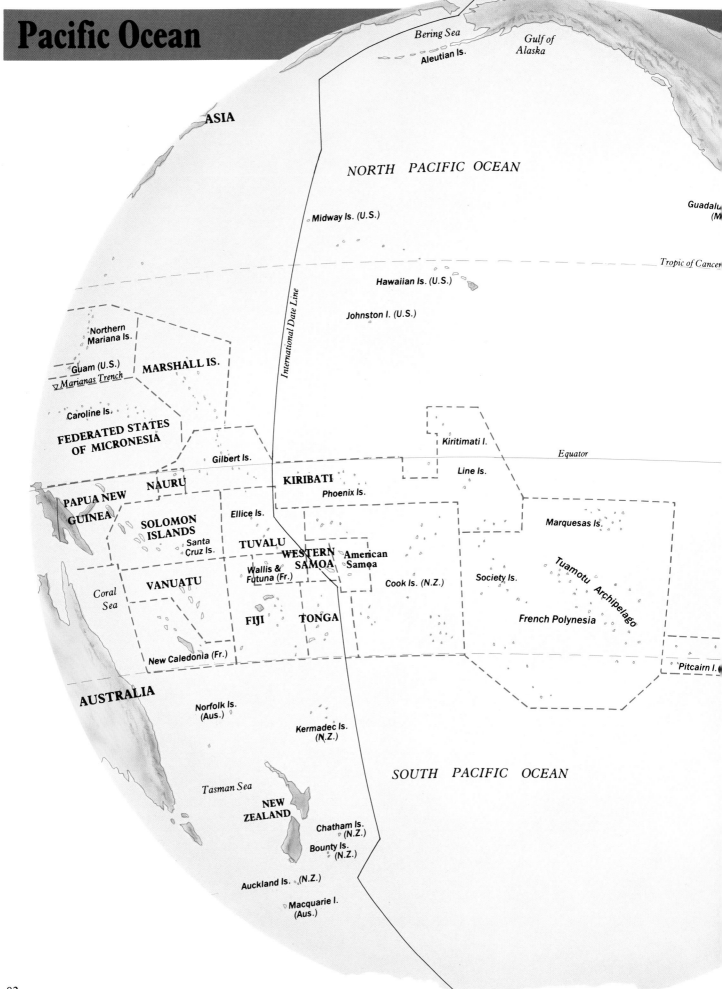

Pacific Ocean

Bering Sea

Gulf of Alaska

Aleutian Is.

ASIA

NORTH   PACIFIC   OCEAN

Guadalu (M

Midway Is. (U.S.)

Tropic of Cancer

Hawaiian Is. (U.S.)

Johnston I. (U.S.)

Northern Mariana Is.

Guam (U.S.)

▽Marianas Trench

MARSHALL IS.

International Date Line

Caroline Is.

FEDERATED STATES OF MICRONESIA

Kiritimati I.

Equator

Line Is.

Gilbert Is.

KIRIBATI

NAURU

Phoenix Is.

Marquesas Is.

PAPUA NEW GUINEA

SOLOMON ISLANDS

Ellice Is.

Santa Cruz Is.

TUVALU

WESTERN SAMOA

American Samoa

Society Is.

Tuamotu Archipelago

Coral Sea

VANUATU

Wallis & Futuna (Fr.)

Cook Is. (N.Z.)

French Polynesia

FIJI

TONGA

New Caledonia (Fr.)

Pitcairn I.

AUSTRALIA

Norfolk Is. (Aus.)

Kermadec Is. (N.Z.)

SOUTH   PACIFIC   OCEAN

Tasman Sea

NEW ZEALAND

Chatham Is. (N.Z.)

Bounty Is. (N.Z.)

Auckland Is. (N.Z.)

Macquarie I. (Aus.)

PACIFIC OCEAN

Area: 69,884,500 sq miles
(181,000,000 sq km)

Deepest point:
33,198 ft (11,033 m)
in the Marianas Trench

International Date Line

The international date line runs north-south through the central Pacific Ocean. When crossing the line from east to west, travelers lose one day. When crossing from west to east, they gain a day.

There is a 24-hour difference between the time on either side of the line. The line does not follow 180° longitude exactly. It bends around islands to avoid confusion.

FEDERATED STATES OF MICRONESIA

Area: 271 sq miles (702 sq km)
Population: 108,000
Capital: Palikir

MARSHALL ISLANDS

Area: 70 sq miles (181 sq km)
Population: 43,000
Capital: Majuro

NAURU

Area: 8 sq miles (21 sq km)
Population: 9,000
Capital: Yaren

KIRIBATI

Area: 281 sq miles (728 sq km)
Population: 71,000
Capital: Bairiki (on Tarawa)

TUVALU

Area: 10 sq miles (25 sq km)
Population: 9,000
Capital: Fongafale (on Funafuti atoll)

WESTERN SAMOA

Area: 1,097 sq miles (2,842 sq km)
Population: 165,000
Capital: Apia

FIJI

Area: 7,056 sq miles (18,274 sq km)
Population: 740,000
Capital: Suva

TONGA

Area: 270 sq miles (699 sq km)
Population: 96,000
Capital: Nuku'alofa

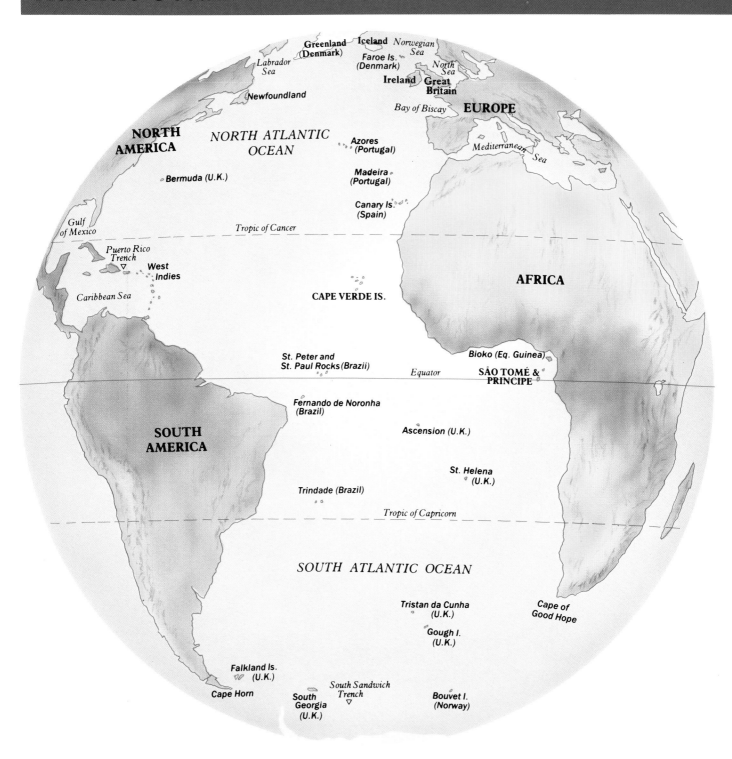

Greenland
(Denmark)

Iceland

*Norwegian
Sea*

*Labrador
Sea*

Faroe Is.
(Denmark)

*North
Sea*

Newfoundland

Ireland **Great
Britain**

**NORTH
AMERICA**

*NORTH ATLANTIC
OCEAN*

Bay of Biscay **EUROPE**

Azores
(Portugal)

Mediterranean Sea

• Bermuda (U.K.)

Madeira
(Portugal)

*Gulf
of Mexico*

Canary Is.
(Spain)

AFRICA

Tropic of Cancer

*Puerto Rico
Trench*
▽   **West
Indies**

Caribbean Sea

CAPE VERDE IS.

St. Peter and
St. Paul Rocks (Brazil)

Bioko (Eq. Guinea)

Equator **SÃO TOMÉ &
PRINCIPE**

Fernando de Noronha
(Brazil)

Ascension (U.K.)

**SOUTH
AMERICA**

St. Helena
(U.K.)

Trindade (Brazil)

Tropic of Capricorn

SOUTH ATLANTIC OCEAN

Tristan da Cunha
(U.K.)

*Cape of
Good Hope*

Gough I.
(U.K.)

Falkland Is.
(U.K.)

*South Sandwich
Trench*
▽

Bouvet I.
(Norway)

Cape Horn

South
Georgia
(U.K.)

ATLANTIC OCEAN

Area: 31,467,330 sq miles
(81,500,000 sq km)

Deepest point: 30,250 ft (9,220 m)
in the Puerto Rico Trench

INDIAN OCEAN

Area: 28,571,560 sq miles
(74,000,000 sq km)

Deepest point: 24,442 ft (7,450 m)
in the Java Trench

ASIA

Gulf of Oman

Tropic of Cancer

Arabian Sea

Red Sea

Laccadive Is.
(India)

Bay of Bengal

Andaman Is.
(India)

*Andaman
Sea*

Socotra
(Yemen)

SRI
LANKA

Nicobar Is.
(India)

MALDIVES

Equator

Sumatra

AFRICA

Chagos
Archipelago
(Seychelles)

Java Trench ▽

Java

Zanzibar

SEYCHELLES

Christmas I. (Aus.)

Cocos Is.
(Aus.)

COMORO
IS.

Rodrigues I. (Maur.)

MADAGASCAR

MAURITIUS

Tropic of Capricorn

Réunion
(France)

AUSTRALIA

*Mozambique
Channel*

I N D I A N   O C E A N

Amsterdam I. (Fr.)

St. Paul I. (Fr.)

Cape of
Good Hope

Crozet Is.
(France)

Kerguelen Is.
(France)

Prince
Edward Is.
(S. Africa)

Heard I. (Aus.)

ANTARCTICA

MALDIVES
Area: 115 sq miles (298 sq km)
Population: 214,000
Capital: Male

SEYCHELLES
Area: 156 sq miles (404 sq km)
Population: 69,000
Capital: Victoria

MAURITIUS
Area: 720 sq miles (1,865 sq km)
Population: 1,080,000
Capital: Port Louis

Arctic Ocean

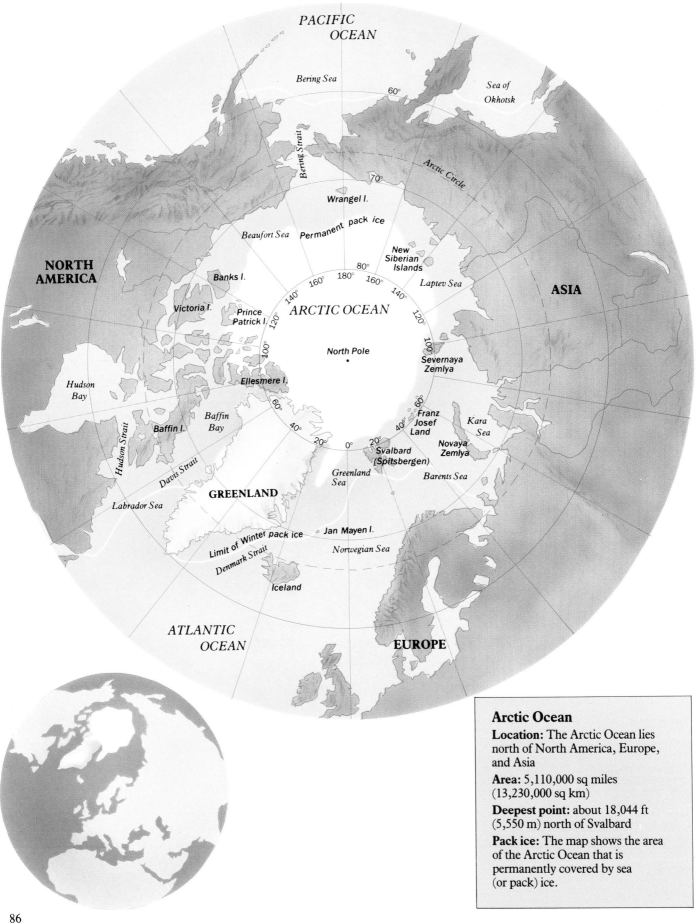

PACIFIC OCEAN

Bering Sea

60°

Sea of Okhotsk

Bering Strait

Arctic Circle

70°

Wrangel I.

Beaufort Sea

Permanent pack ice

New Siberian Islands

Banks I.

80°

Laptev Sea

ASIA

160° 180° 160°

140° 140°

Victoria I.

ARCTIC OCEAN

120°

NORTH AMERICA

Prince Patrick I.

120°

100°

North Pole

100°

Severnaya Zemlya

Ellesmere I.

60°

60°

Hudson Bay

Franz Josef Land

Kara Sea

40°

Baffin I.

Baffin Bay

40°

Novaya Zemlya

Hudson Strait

20°

Svalbard (Spitsbergen)

Barents Sea

Davis Strait

0°

Greenland Sea

GREENLAND

Labrador Sea

Jan Mayen I.

Limit of Winter pack ice

Norwegian Sea

Denmark Strait

Iceland

ATLANTIC OCEAN

EUROPE

Arctic Ocean

Location: The Arctic Ocean lies north of North America, Europe, and Asia

Area: 5,110,000 sq miles (13,230,000 sq km)

Deepest point: about 18,044 ft (5,550 m) north of Svalbard

Pack ice: The map shows the area of the Arctic Ocean that is permanently covered by sea (or pack) ice.

Antarctica

Location: Antarctica is a frozen continent at the South Pole. The waters around Antarctica are sometimes called the Antarctic Ocean, but most geographers consider these waters to be part of the Pacific, Atlantic, and Indian oceans.

Area: About 5,405,400 sq miles (about 14,000,000 sq km)

Population: None permanent

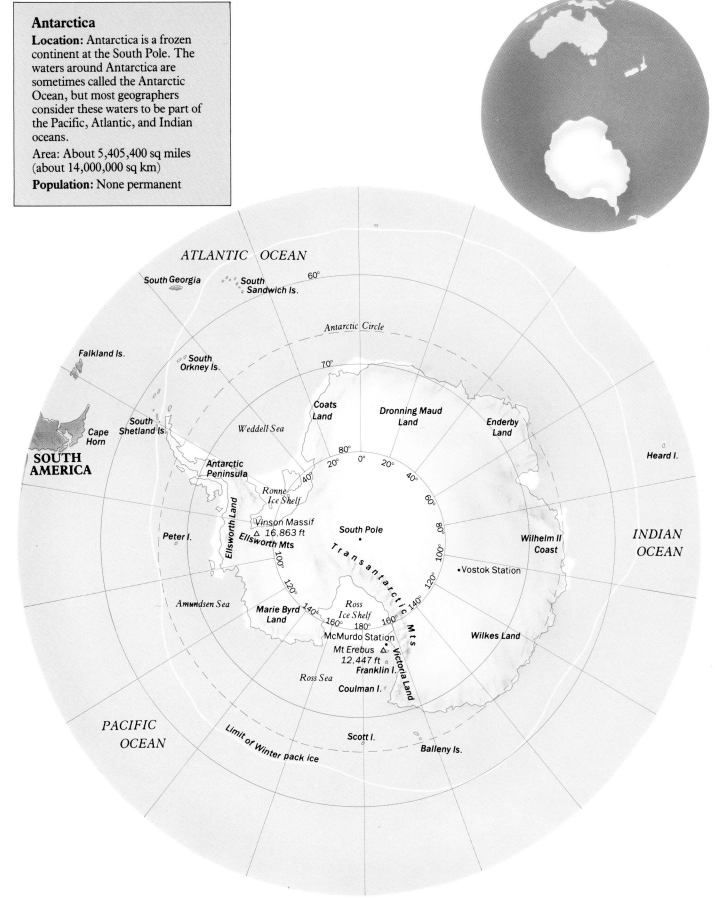

ATLANTIC OCEAN

South Georgia
South Sandwich Is.
60°

Antarctic Circle

Falkland Is.
South Orkney Is.
70°

Coats Land
Dronning Maud Land
Enderby Land

South Shetland Is.
Weddell Sea
80°
20°
0°
20°
40°
60°

Heard I.

Cape Horn

SOUTH AMERICA

Antarctic Peninsula
Ronne Ice Shelf
40°

Ellsworth Land

Peter I.

Vinson Massif
△ 16,863 ft
Ellsworth Mts

South Pole

80°

Wilhelm II Coast

INDIAN OCEAN

100°

• Vostok Station

Amundsen Sea
120°
140°
160°
180°
160°
140°
120°

Marie Byrd Land

Ross Ice Shelf

Transantarctic Mts

Wilkes Land

McMurdo Station •
Mt Erebus △
12,447 ft
Franklin I.
Victoria Land

Ross Sea
Coulman I.

PACIFIC OCEAN

Limit of Winter pack ice

Scott I.

Balleny Is.

Index

Bijagos Is. 72 C4
Bikaner 63 C3
Bilaspur 63 E4
Bilbao 47 D1
Billings 29 F1
Biloxi 25 E2
Binga, Mt. 76 C2
Binghamton 23 F3
Bioko I. 74 A1
Birjand 61 E2
Birkenhead 45 E4
Birmingham (AL) 25 E2
Birmingham (U.K.) 45 F4
Biscay, Bay of 42 C4
Bishkek 54 C2
Bismarck 26 A1
Bismarck Sea 80 D1
Bissau 72 C4
Bitola 53 D3
Biysk 55 D2
Black Forest 50 B2
Black Hills 26 A2
Blackpool 45 E4
Black Sea 53 F2
Black Volta 73 F4
Blackwater R. 44 B4
Blagoveshchensk 55 F2
Blanc, Mt. 43 G4
Blantyre 76 C2
Blida 70 C1
Bloemfontein 76 B3
Blois 42 D3
Bloomington (IL) 27 D2
Bloomington (IN) 27 D3
Bluefield 22 D5
Blue Nile 71 F3
Blue Ridge Mts. 25 F1
Blumenau 37 E5
Blyth 45 F3
Bo 72 D5
Boa Vista I. 72 B1
Bobo Dioulasso 73 F4
Bobonong 76 B2
Boden 48 H3
Bodmin Moor 45 D5
Bodø 48 F2
Bogor 66 B4
Bogotá 36 B2
Bo Hai Sea 65 D2
Bohemian Forest 50 C2
Bohol 67 D3
Boise 29 D2
Bolivia 36 C4
Bologna 52 B2
Bolzano 52 B1
Bombay 63 C5
Bomu R. 74 B1
Bonaire 33 D4
Bong Range 72 D5
Bonn 50 B2
Borås 48 F5
Bordeaux 42 C4
Borger 24 B1
Borlänge 48 F4
Borneo 67 C3
Bornholm 48 F5
Borujerd 60 C2
Bosna R. 53 D2
Bosnia and Hercegovina 52 C2
Bosporus 58 B1
Boston (MA) 23 H3
Boston (U.K.) 45 F4
Bothnia, Gulf of 48 H3
Botosani 53 F1
Botswana 76 B2
Bouaké 72 F5
Bouar 74 B1
Bougainville I. 80 E1
Boulder 29 F2
Boulogne 42 D1
Bounty Is. 82

Bourg-en-Bresse 43 F3
Bourges 42 E3
Bourke 80 D4
Bournemouth 45 F5
Bouvet I. 84
Bowling Green 22 B5
Bowman 26 A1
Boyoma Falls 74 C1
Bozeman 29 E1
Bradenton 25 F3
Bradford 45 F4
Braga 46 A2
Braganca 46 B2
Brahmaputra R. 63 G3
Braila 53 F2
Branco R. 36 C2
Brandon 19 C3
Brasilia 36 E4
Brasov 53 E2
Bratislava 50 D2
Bratsk 55 E2
Brattleboro 23 G2
Braunschweig 50 C1
Brava 72 B2
Brazil 36 D3
Brazilian Highlands 36 E4
Brazos R. 24 C2
Brazzaville 74 B2
Breda 50 A2
Bremen 50 B1
Bremerhaven 50 B1
Bremerton 28 C1
Brescia 52 B2
Brest (Belarus) 54 A2
Brest (France) 42 A2
Bridgeport 23 G3
Bridgetown 33 F4
Bridgwater 45 E5
Bridlington 45 F3
Brig 43 G3
Brigham City 29 E2
Brighton 45 F5
Brindisi 53 C3
Brisbane 80 E3
Bristol 45 E5
British Columbia 18 A3
Brno 50 D2
Brockton 23 H3
Broken Bow 26 B2
Broken Hill 80 D4
Brookings 26 B2
Brooks Range 28 B1
Broome 80 B2
Brownsville 24 C3
Bruges 42 E1
Brunei 67 C3
Brunswick 25 F2
Brussels 43 F1
Bryan 24 C2
Bucaramanga 36 B2
Buchanan 72 D5
Bucharest 53 F2
Buckie 45 E2
Bucksport 23 I2
Budapest 51 E3
Buenaventura 36 B2
Buenos Aires 37 D6
Buffalo 22 E2
Bug R. 51 F1
Bujumbura 74 C2
Bukavu 74 C2
Bulawayo 76 B2
Bulgaria 53 E2
Bunbury 80 A4
Bundaberg 80 E3
Buraydah 60 B3
Burgas 53 F2
Burgos 46 D1
Burhanpur 63 D4
Burkina Faso 73 F4
Burlington (IA) 27 C2

Burlington (VT) 23 G2
Burma See Myanmar
Bursa 58 B1
Burton 45 F4
Buru 67 D4
Burundi 75 C2
Bushire 60 D3
Busra 59 D3
Butan 67 D3
Butte 29 E1
Buzau 53 F2
Bydgoszcz 50 D1

C
Cabimas 36 B1
Cabinda 74 A2
Cabora Bassa Dam 76 C2
Cabrera 47 G3
Cacak 53 D2
Cáceres 46 B3
Cadiz (Philippines) 67 D2
Cádiz (Spain) B4
Caen 42 C2
Caernarfon 45 D4
Cagayan de Oro 67 D3
Cagliari 52 A3
Cairns 80 D2
Cairo 71 F1
Calabar 73 H6
Calais 42 D1
Calcutta 63 F4
Calgary 18 B3
Cali 36 B2
Calicut 63 D6
California 28 D3
California, Gulf of 30 B2
Callao 36 B4
Caloocan 67 D2
Caltanissetta 52 C4
Camagüey 32 B2
Camagüey Arch. 32 B2
Cambodia 66 B2
Cambrian Mts. 45 E4
Cambridge (MA) 23 H3
Cambridge (U.K.) 45 G4
Camden 23 F4
Cameroon 74 A1
Cameroon, Mt. 74 A1
Campeche 31 F4
Campeche Bay 31 F4
Campinas 37 E5
Campo Grande 36 D5
Campos 37 E5
Cam Ranh 66 B2
Canada 18
Canadian R. 24 B1
Canakkale 58 A1
Canal du Midi 42 E5
Canary Is. 46 I5
Canberra 80 D4
Cancer, Tropic of 12
Cankiri 59 C1
Canna 45 C2
Cannes 43 G5
Cantabrian Mts. 46 C1
Canterbury 45 G5
Can Tho 66 B3
Canton (MS) 24 E2
Canton (OH) 27 E2
Cape Canaveral 25 F3
Cape Coast 73 F5
Cape Cod 23 I3
Cape Girardeau 27 D3
Cape Horn 37 C8
Cape May 23 G4
Cape of Good Hope 76 A3
Cape Town 76 A3
Cape Verde Is. 72 A1
Cap-Haïtien 33 C3
Capri 52 C3
Capricorn, Tropic of 12

Caprivi Strip 76 B2
Caracas 36 C1
Carcassonne 42 E5
Cardiff 45 E5
Caribbean Sea 32 B3
Caribou 23 I1
Carlisle 45 E3
Carlsbad 29 G4
Carmarthen 45 D5
Carnarvon 80 A3
Caroline Is. 82
Carpathian Mts. 51 E2
Carpentaria, Gulf of 80 C2
Carrauntoohill, Mt. 44 B4
Carrick-on-Shannon 44 B4
Carson City 28 D3
Cartagena (Colombia) 36 B1
Cartagena (Spain) 47 E4
Carthage 26 C3
Casablanca 70 B1
Cascade Range 28 C1
Casper 29 F2
Caspian Sea 54 B2
Castellón 47 E3
Castelo Branco 46 B3
Castlebar 44 B4
Castries 33 E4
Catalonia 47 F1
Catania 52 C4
Catanzaro 52 C3
Cat I. 32 B2
Catskill Mts. 23 G3
Cavally R. 72 E5
Cavan 44 C4
Cayenne 36 D2
Cayman Islands 32 A3
Cebu 67 D2
Cedar City 29 E3
Cedar Falls 26 C2
Cedar Rapids 27 C2
Celaya 30 D3
Celebes, see Sulawesi
Celebes Sea 67 D3
Central African Republic 74 B1
Central Siberian Plateau 55 E1
Ceram 67 D4
Ceram Sea 67 D4
České Budějovice 50 D2
Ceuta 70 B1
Ceyhan R. 59 D2
Chad 71 D3
Chad, L. 70 D3
Chagos Arch. 85
Chah Bahar 61 F3
Châlon-sur-Saône 43 F3
Chambersburg 23 E4
Chambéry 43 F4
Champaign 27 D2
Champlain L. 23 G2
Chandigarh 63 D2
Changchun 65 E2
Chang Jiang (Yangtze River) 64 D3
Changsha 65 D3
Channel Is. 45 H5
Channel Is. (USA) 28 D4
Chari R. 70 D3
Charleroi 43 F1
Charleston (SC) 25 G2
Charleston (WV) 22 D4
Charleville-Mézières 43 F2
Charlotte 25 F1
Charlotte Amalie 33 D3
Charlottesville 23 E4
Charlottetown 19 D3
Chartres 42 D2
Châteauroux 42 D3
Châtellerault 42 D3
Chatham 45 G5
Chatham Is. 82
Chattahoochee R. 25 F2
Chattanooga 25 E1

Chaumont 43 F2
Cheju 65 E2
Chelmsford 45 G5
Cheltenham 45 E5
Chelyabinsk 54 C2
Chemnitz 50 C2
Chengdu 64 C3
Cherbourg 42 C2
Cheremkhovo 55 E2
Chernovtsy 54 A2
Cher R. 42 E3
Chesapeake Bay 23 F5
Chester 45 E4
Chesterfield 45 F4
Chesuncook L. 23 I1
Cheyenne 29 G2
Cheyenne R. 26 A2
Chiang Mai 66 A2
Chiba 65 F2
Chicago 27 D2
Chickamauga L. 25 F1
Chiclayo 36 B3
Chico 28 C3
Chihuahua 30 C2
Chile 37 B5
Chillán 37 B6
Chilterns 45 E5
Chilung 65 E3
Chimborazo, Mt. 36 B3
Chimbote 36 B3
Chimoio 76 C2
China 64 C2
Chingola 76 B1
Chita 55 E2
Chitral 63 C1
Chittagong 63 G4
Chon Buri 66 B2
Chongjin 65 E2
Chongqing 64 C3
Chorzów 51 E2
Christchurch 81 G5
Christmas I. 85
Chubut R. 37 C7
Chur 43 H3
Churchill 19 C3
Churchill R. 19 C3
Ciego de Avila 32 B2
Cienfuegos 32 A2
Cimarron R. 24 C1
Cincinnati 27 E3
Cinto, Mt. 43 H5
Citlaltépetl Volcano 30 E4
Ciudad Bolivar 36 C2
Ciudad Guayana 36 C2
Ciudad Juárez 30 C1
Ciudad Obrêgon 30 C2
Ciudad Real 46 D3
Ciudad Victoria 30 E3
Clacton-on-Sea 45 G5
Claremont 23 H2
Clark Fork R. 29 D1
Clarksburg 22 D4
Clarksville 25 E1
Clearwater 25 F3
Clermont-Ferrand 42 E4
Cleveland 27 E2
Clinton 24 C1
Clipperton I. 83
Clovis 29 G4
Cluj-Napoca 53 E1
Clyde R. 45 E3
Coast Mts. 18 A3
Coast Ranges 28 C2
Coats Land 87
Coatzacoalcos 31 F4
Cobh 44 B5
Cochabamba 36 C4
Cochin 63 D7
Coco, Isla del 83
Cocoa 25 F3

Cocos Is. 85
Cognac 42 C4
Coimbatore 63 D6
Coimbra 46 A2
Colchester 45 G5
Coleraine 45 C3
Colima 30 D4
Coll 45 C2
Colmar 43 G2
Cologne 50 B2
Colombia 36 B2
Colombo 63 D7
Colón (Cuba) 32 A2
Colón (Panama) 31 I6
Colonsay 45 C2
Colorado 29 F3
Colorado Plateau 29 E3
Colorado R. (Argentina) 37 C6
Colorado R. (TX) 24 C3
Colorado Springs 29 G3
Columbia 26 C3
Columbia Plateau 28 D2
Columbia R. 28 C1
Columbia (SC) 25 F2
Columbia (TN) 25 E1
Columbus (GA) 25 F2
Columbus (MS) 25 E2
Columbus (OH) 27 E3
Communism Peak 54 C3
Como 52 A2
Comodoro Rivadavia 37 C7
Como L. 52 A2
Comoros Is. 77 D1
Conakry 72 D5
Concepción (Chile) 37 B6
Concepción (Paraguay) 37 D5
Concord 23 H2
Congo 74 C2
Connecticut 23 G3
Connecticut R. 23 H2
Conn, Lough 44 B3
Consett 45 F3
Constance L. 43 H3
Constanța 53 F2
Constantine 70 C1
Cook Is. 82
Cook, Mt. 81 G5
Cook Strait 81 G5
Cooktown 80 D2
Coos Bay 28 C2
Copenhagen 48 F5
Copper Harbor 27 D1
Coppermine 18 B2
Coral Sea 80 E2
Córdoba (Argentina) 37 C6
Córdoba (Spain) 46 C4
Corfu 53 D3
Cork 44 B5
Corner Brook 19 E3
Corno Mt. 52 B2
Corpus Christi 24 C3
Corrib Lough 44 B4
Corrientes 37 D5
Corsica 43 H5
Corum 59 C1
Corumbá 36 D4
Corvallis 28 C2
Cosenza 52 C3
Costa Rica 31 H5
Côte d'Ivoire (Ivory Coast) 72 E5
Cotonou 73 G5
Cotswolds 45 E5
Cottbus 50 D2
Coulman I. 87
Council Bluffs 26 B2
Coventry 45 F4
Covilhã 46 B2
Covington 22 C4
Craiova 53 E2
Creil 42 E2
Cremona 52 B2

Gotland 48 G5
Gough I. 84
Governador Valadares 36 E4
Grafton 80 E3
Grampian Mts. 45 E2
Granada (Nicaragua) 31 G5
Granada (Spain) 46 D4
Gran Canaria 46 J6
Gran Chaco 37 C5
Grand Bahama I. 32 B1
Grand Canyon 29 E3
Grand Coulee Dam 29 D1
Grand Forks 26 B1
Grand Island 26 B2
Grand Junction 29 F3
Grand Rapids 27 D2
Grand Turk 33 C2
Grantham 45 F4
Granville 42 C2
Graz 50 D3
Great Abaco I. 32 B1
Great Artesian Basin 80 D3
Great Australian Bight 80 B4
Great Barrier Reef 80 D2
Great Basin 29 D3
Great Bear L. 18 B2
Great Bend 26 B3
Great Dividing Range 80 D4
Greater Antilles 32 B3
Great Exuma I. 32 B2
Great Falls 29 E1
Great Inagua I. 33 C2
Great Karroo 76 B3
Great Ouse R. 45 G4
Great Plains 29 F1
Great Rift Valley 71 F4
Great Salt Lake 29 E2
Great Sandy Desert 80 B3
Great Slave Lake 18 B2
Great Victoria Desert 80 B3
Great Wall of China 64 D2
Great Yarmouth 45 G4
Greece 53 E3
Greeley 29 G2
Green Bay 27 D2
Greenland 19 E2
Greenland Sea 86
Greenock 45 D3
Greensboro 25 G1
Greenville (MS) 24 D2
Greenville (SC) 25 F2
Grenada 33 E4
Grenoble 43 F4
Gretna Green 45 E3
Grimsby 45 F4
Groningen 50 B1
Gross Glockner 50 C3
Groznyy 54 B2
Guadalajara (Mexico) 30 D3
Guadalajara (Spain) 47 D2
Guadalcanal I. 81 F1
Guadalquivir R. 46 C4
Guadalupe I. 82
Guadalupe Peak 24 B2
Guadeloupe 33 E3
Guadiana R. 46 C3
Guam 82
Guanabacoa 32 A2
Guane 32 A2
Guangzhou 65 D3
Guantánamo 32 B2
Guasav 30 C2
Guatemala 31 F4
Guatemala City 31 F5
Guaviare R. 36 C2
Guayaquil 36 B3
Guernsey 45 H5
Guiana Highlands 36 C2
Guildford 45 F5
Guilin 64 D3
Guinea 72 D4

Guinea-Bissau 72 D4
Güines 32 A2
Guiyang 64 C3
Gujranwala 63 C2
Gulf, The 60 D3
Gulfport 25 E2
Gulu 75 C1
Gunnbjorn, Mt 19 F2
Guntur 63 E5
Gusau 73 H4
Guyana 36 D2
Gwadar 62 A3
Gwalior 63 D3
Gweru 76 B2
Gyandzha 54 B2
Györ 50 D3

H
Haarlem 50 A1
Hadejia R. 73 I4
Hadhramaut 60 C5
Hafar 60 C3
Hafnarfjördhur 48 A2
Hagerstown 23 E4
Hague, The 50 A1
Haifa 59 C3
Haikou 64 D4
Hail 60 B3
Hainan 64 D4
Haiphong 66 B1
Haiti 33 C3
Hakodate 65 F2
Halberstadt 50 C2
Halifax (Canada) 19 D3
Halifax (U.K.) 45 F4
Halle 50 C2
Halmahera 67 D3
Halmstad 48 F5
Hama 59 D3
Hamadan 60 C2
Hamamatsu 65 F2
Hamar 48 E4
Hamburg 50 C1
Hämeenlinna 48 I4
Hamhung 65 E2
Hamilton (Canada) 19 D3
Hamilton (New Zealand) 81 G4
Hamilton (OH) 27 E3
Hamilton (U.K.) 45 D3
Hammerfest 48 H1
Hampton 23 F5
Handan 65 D2
Hangzhou 65 E3
Hanoi 66 B1
Hanover 50 B1
Haradh 60 C4
Harar 71 G4
Harare 76 C2
Harbin 65 E1
Hardanger Plateau 48 D4
Hargeisa 71 G4
Härnösand 48 G3
Harrisburg 23 F3
Harrison 24 D1
Harrisonburg 23 E4
Harrogate 45 F4
Harstad 48 G2
Hartford 23 G3
Hartlepool 45 F3
Harz Mts. 50 C2
Hasselt 43 F1
Hastings (NE) 26 B2
Hastings (New Zealand) 81 G4
Hastings (U.K.) 45 G5
Hatteras, Cape 25 G1
Hattiesburg 25 E2
Hat Yai 66 B3
Haugesund 48 D4
Havana 32 A2
Havre 29 F1
Hawaii 28 A1
Hawaiian Is. 82

Hawick 45 E3
Hays 26 B3
Heard I. 85
Hebron 59 C4
Hefei 65 D3
Heidelberg 50 B2
Heilbronn 50 B2
Heimaey I. 48 A2
Hejaz 60 A4
Helena 29 E1
Helsingborg 48 F5
Helsinki 48 I4
Hengyang 65 D3
Herat 62 A2
Hereford 45 E4
Hermosillo 30 B2
Herning 48 E5
Hidalgo Del Parral 30 C2
Hierro 46 I6
High Atlas Mts. 70 B1
High Point 25 G1
Hilo 28 A1
Himalayas 63 D2, 64 B3
Hindu Kush 62 B2
Hinggan Range, Greater 65 D1
Hinggan Range, Lesser 65 E1
Hiroshima 65 F2
Ho 73 G5
Hobart 80 D5
Ho Chi Minh City 66 B2
Hódmezövásárhely 51 E3
Hofn 48 C2
Hohhot 65 D2
Hokkaido 65 F2
Holguin 32 B2
Holon 59 C3
Holstebro 48 E5
Holyhead 45 D4
Holy I. 45 F3
Homs 59 D3
Honduras 31 G5
Honduras, Gulf of 31 G4
Hong Kong 65 D3
Honiara 81 E1
Honolulu 28 A1
Honshu 65 F2
Hoover Dam 29 E3
Hopkinsville 22 B5
Hormuz, Strait of 61 E3
Hospitalet 47 G2
Hot Springs 24 D2
Houston 24 D2
Hovsgol L. 64 C1
Howrah 63 F4
Hradec Králové 50 D2
Huainan 65 D2
Huambo 74 B3
Huancayo 36 B4
Huang He R. 64 C2
Huangshi 65 D3
Huascaran, Mt. 36 B3
Hubli 63 D5
Huddersfield 45 F4
Hudson Bay 19 C3
Hudson R. 23 G3
Hudson Strait 19 D2
Hue 66 B2
Huelva 46 B4
Huesca 47 E1
Hull 19 D3
Humber R. 45 F4
Humboldt R. 28 D2
Hungary 51 E3
Huntington 22 D4
Huntsville 25 E2
Huron 26 B2
Huron L. 19 C3
Hutchinson 26 B3
Hvannadalshnúkur, Mt. 48 B2
Hyderabad (India) 63 D5
Hyderabad (Pakistan) 62 B3

I
Iaşi 53 F1
Ibadan 73 G5
Ibagué 36 B2
Ibiza 47 F3
Ica 36 B4
Iceland 48 B2
Idaho 29 E2
Idaho Falls 29 E2
Ife 73 G5
IJsselmeer 50 A1
Ikaria 53 F4
Ilebo 74 B2
Ilesha 73 G5
Ilhéus 36 F4
Iligan 67 D3
Illinois 27 D3
Illinois R. 27 C2
Iloilo 67 D2
Ilorin 73 G5
Imphal 63 G4
Inari 48 I2
Inchon 65 E2
Independence 26 C3
India 63 D4
Indiana 27 D2
Indianapolis 27 D3
Indian Ocean 85
Indigirka R. 55 G1
Indonesia 67 C4
Indore 63 D4
Indus R. 62 B3
Inhambane 76 C2
Inner Hebrides 45 C2
Inn R. 50 C2
Innsbruck 50 C3
Inowrocław 50 E1
International Date Line 82
International Falls 26 C1
Invercargill 81 F5
Inverness 45 D2
Ioannina 53 D3
Iona 45 C2
Ionian Sea 53 D3
Iowa 26 C2
Iowa City 27 C2
Ipoh 66 B3
Ipswich (Australia) 80 E3
Ipswich (U.K.) 45 G4
Iquique 36 B4
Iquitos 36 B3
Iran 61 D2
Irapuato 30 D3
Iraq 60 B2
Irbid 59 C3
Irbil 60 B1
Ireland, Republic of 44 C4
Irian Jaya 67 E4
Iringa 75 D2
Irish Sea 45 D4
Irkutsk 55 E2
Ironwood 27 C1
Irrawaddy R. 66 A2
Irtysh R. 54 C2
Irún 47 E1
Isafjördhur 48 A1
Ischia 52 B3
Isère R. 43 F4
Iskenderun 59 D2
Islamabad 63 C2
Islay 45 C3
Isparta 58 B2
Israel 59 C3
Istanbul 58 B1
Italy 52 B2
Ithaca 23 F3
Ivanovo 54 B2
Iwo 73 G5
Izhevsk 54 B2
Izmir 58 A2

Izmit 58 B1

J
Jabalpur 63 D4
Jackson (MS) 24 D2
Jackson (TN) 25 E1
Jacksonville (FL) 25 F2
Jacksonville (NC) 25 G2
Jacmel 33 C3
Jaén 46 D4
Jaffna 63 E7
Jaipur 63 D3
Jakarta 66 B4
Jalalabad 62 C2
Jalapa Enriquez 30 E4
Jamaica 32 B3
Jambi 66 B4
James Bay 19 C3
James R. (SD) 26 B2
James R. (VA) 23 E4
Jamestown (ND) 26 B1
Jamestown (NY) 22 E3
Jammu 63 C2
Jamnagar 62 B4
Jamshedpur 63 F4
Janesville 27 D2
Jan Mayen I. 86
Japan 65 F2
Japan, Sea of 65 F2
Japurá R. 36 B3
Jardines de la Reina 32 B2
Jarosław 51 F2
Java 66 B4
Java Sea 67 C4
Java Trench 85
Jebel Marra, Mt. 71 E3
Jefferson City 26 C3
Jérémie 32 C3
Jersey 45 H5
Jersey City 23 G3
Jerusalem 59 C4
Jhansi 63 D3
Jiddah 60 A4
Jihlava 50 D2
Jilin 65 E2
Jinan 65 D2
Jingdezhen 65 D3
Jinja 75 C1
Jinzhou 65 E2
Jixi 65 E1
Jizan 60 B5
João Pessoa 36 F3
Jodhpur 63 C3
Joensuu 49 J3
Johannesburg 76 B3
John Day River 28 C1
John o'Groats 45 E1
Johnson City 25 F1
Johnston I. 82
Johnstown 22 E3
Johor Baharu 66 B3
Jonesboro 24 D1
Jönköping 48 F5
Joplin 26 C3
Jordan 59 D4
Jordan R. 59 C3
Jos Plateau 73 H4
Jostedal Glacier 48 D4
Juan Fernández Is. 37 B6
Juba 71 F4
Juiz de Fora 37 E5
Jullundur 63 D2
Junction City 26 B3
Juneau 28 B1
Jura 45 D3
Jura Mts. 43 G3
Juruá R. 36 C3
Jutland 48 E5
Jyväskylä 49 I3

K
K2 Mt. 63 D1
Kabalo 74 C2
Kabul 62 B2
Kabwe 76 B1
Kaduna 73 H4
Kafue R. 76 B2
Kagoshima 65 E3
Kahoolawe 28 A1
Kaifeng 65 D2
Kainji L. 73 G4
Kajaani 49 I3
Kalahari Desert 76 B2
Kalamata 53 E4
Kalamazoo 27 D2
Kalat 62 B3
Kalémié 74 C2
Kalgoorlie 80 B4
Kalimantan 67 C4
Kaliningrad 54 A2
Kalispell 29 E1
Kalisz 50 D2
Kallavesi L. 49 I3
Kalmar 48 G5
Kamchatka Peninsula 55 G2
Kamina 74 B2
Kampala 75 C1
Kananga 74 B2
Kanazawa 65 F2
Kandahar 62 B2
Kandy 63 E7
Kangaroo I. 80 C4
Kankakee 27 D2
Kankan 72 E4
Kannapolis 25 F1
Kano 73 H4
Kanpur 63 E3
Kansas 26 B3
Kansas City (KS) 26 C3
Kansas City (MO) 26 C3
Kansas R. 26 B3
Kaolack 72 C4
Karachi 62 B4
Karaganda 54 C2
Karakoram Range 63 D1
Karaman 59 C2
Kara Kum Desert 54 C3
Kara Sea 55 C1
Karbala 60 B2
Kariba Dam 76 B2
Kariba L. 76 B2
Karlskrona 48 F5
Karlsruhe 50 B2
Karlstad 48 F4
Karpathos 53 F4
Kars 59 E1
Kasai R. 74 B2
Kasama 76 C1
Kashan 60 D2
Kashi 64 A2
Kassala 71 F3
Kassel 50 B2
Katahdin, Mt. 23 I1
Katmandu 63 F3
Katowice 51 E2
Katsina 73 H4
Kattegat 48 E5
Kauai 28 A1
Kavalla 53 E3
Kawasaki 65 F2
Kayes 70 A3
Kayseri 59 C2
Kazakhstan 54 C2
Kazan 54 B2
Kebnekaise, Mt. 48 G2
Kecskemét 51 E3
Keetmanshoop 76 A3
Kefallinia 53 D3
Keflavik 48 A2
Kelang 66 B3
Kelkit R. 59 D1

Orsk 54 B2
Orumiyeh 60 B1
Oruro 36 C4
Osaka 65 F2
Oshawa 19 D3
Oshkosh 27 D2
Oshogbo 73 G5
Osijek 53 D2
Oskaloosa 26 C2
Oslo 48 E4
Osmaniye 59 D2
Osnabrück 50 B1
Osorno 37 B7
Ossa, Mt. 80 D5
Ostend 42 E1
Ostersund 48 F3
Ostrava 50 E2
Oti R. 73 G5
Ottawa 19 D3
Ottawa R. 19 D3
Ottumwa 26 C2
Ouachita Mts. 24 D2
Ouachita R. 24 D2
Ouagadougou 73 F4
Ouahigouya 73 F4
Oujda 70 B1
Oulu 49 I3
Oulujärvi L. 49 I3
Ouse R. 45 F3
Outer Hebrides 44 C2
Oviedo 46 C1
Owensboro 22 B4
Owen Stanley Range 80 D1
Oxford (MS) 25 E2
Oxford (U.K.) 45 F5
Oyo 73 G5
Ozark Plateau 26 C3

P

Paarl 76 A3
Pachuca 30 E3
Pacific Ocean 82
Padang 66 B4
Padua 52 B2
Paducah 22 A5
Päijänne L. 49 I4
Paisley 45 D3
Pakanbaru 66 B3
Pakistan 62 B3
Pakse 66 B2
Palawan 67 C3
Palembang 66 B4
Palencia 46 C1
Palermo 52 B3
Palimé 73 G5
Palma 47 G3
Palmerston North 81 G5
Palmyra 59 D3
Palu 67 C4
Pamir Mts. 54 C3
Pamlico Sound 25 G1
Pampa 37 C6
Pamplona 47 E1
Panama 31 H6
Panama Canal 31 I6
Panama City (FL) 25 E2
Panama City (Panama) 31 I6
Panama, Gulf of 31 I6
Panay 67 D2
Pantelleria 52 B4
Paphos 59 C3
Papua New Guinea 80 D1
Paraguay 37 D5
Paraguay R. 36 D4
Parakou 73 G5
Paramaribo 36 D2
Paraná 37 C6
Paraná R. 37 D5
Pardubice 50 D2
Paris (France) 42 E2
Paris (TX) 24 C2

Parkersburg 22 D4
Parma (Italy) 52 B2
Parma (OH) 27 E2
Parnaiba 36 E3
Pascagoula 25 E2
Passo Fundo 37 D5
Pasto 36 B2
Patagonia 37 C7
Paterson 23 G3
Patiala 63 D2
Patna 63 F3
Patras 53 D3
Pau 42 C5
Pavia 52 A2
Paysandú 37 D6
Peace R. 18 B3
Pearl R. 24 D2
Pec 53 D2
Pecos 24 B2
Pecos R. 24 B2
Pécs 50 E3
Peebles 45 E3
Pee Dee R. 25 G2
Pegu 66 A2
Peipus L. 54 A2
Pekalongan 66 B4
Pelotas 37 D6
Pematangsiantar 66 A3
Pemba 76 D1
Pemba I. 75 D2
Pembroke 45 D5
Pendleton 28 D1
Pennines 45 E3
Pennsylvania 23 F3
Penrith 45 E3
Pensacola 25 E2
Penza 54 B2
Penzance 45 D5
Peoria 27 D2
Pereira 36 B2
Périgueux 42 D4
Perm 54 B2
Pernambuco 42 E5
Pernik 53 E2
Perpignan 42 E5
Perth (Australia) 80 A4
Perth (U.K.) 45 E2
Peru 36 B3
Perugia 52 B2
Pescara 52 C2
Peshawar 63 C2
Peterborough (Canada) 19 D3
Peterborough (U.K.) 45 F4
Peterhead 45 F2
Peter I. 87
Petersburg 23 F5
Petra 59 C4
Petropavlovsk-Kamchatskiy 55 G2
Petrozavodsk 54 A1
Phenix City 25 E2
Philadelphia 23 F3
Philippines 67 D2
Phitsanulok 66 B2
Phnom Penh 66 B2
Phoenix 29 E4
Phoenix Is. 82
Phuket 66 A3
Piacenza 52 A2
Piatra Neamt 53 F1
Piedras Negras 30 D2
Pielinen L. 49 J3
Pierre 26 A2
Pietermaritzburg 76 C3
Pietersburg 76 B2
Pila 51 D1
Pilcomayo R. 37 C5
Pinar del Rio 32 A2
Pindus Mts. 53 D3
Pine Bluff 24 D2
Pine Ridge 26 A2
Pinios R. 53 E3
Piotrków 51 E2

Piraeus 53 E4
Pisa 52 B2
Pitcairn I. 82
Pitesti 53 E2
Pittsburgh 22 E3
Pittsfield 23 G3
Piura 36 A3
Plasencia 46 B2
Platte R. 26 B2
Plattsburgh 23 G2
Plauen 50 C2
Pleven 53 E2
Płock 51 E1
Ploesti 53 F2
Plovdiv 53 E2
Plymouth (Montserrat) 33 E3
Plymouth (U.K.) 45 D5
Plzen 50 C2
Pocatello 29 E2
Pointe Noire 74 A2
Poitiers 42 D3
Pokhara 63 E3
Poland 51 E2
Ponca City 24 C1
Ponce 33 D3
Ponferrada 46 B1
Ponta Grossa 37 D5
Pontchartrain L. 24 D2
Pontevedra 46 A1
Pontiac 27 E2
Pontianak 66 B4
Poole 45 F5
Poopó L. 36 C4
Popayán 36 B2
Poplar Bluff 27 C3
Popocatépetl Volcano 30 E4
Po R. 52 B2
Pori 48 H4
Portadown 45 C3
Port Arthur 24 D3
Port Augusta 80 C4
Port-au-Prince 33 C3
Port Bou 47 G1
Port Elizabeth 76 B3
Port Gentil 74 A2
Port Harcourt 73 H6
Port Hedland 80 A3
Portimão 46 A4
Portland (ME) 23 H2
Portland (OR) 28 C1
Port Laoise 44 C4
Port Moresby 80 D1
Porto 46 A2
Pôrto Alegre 37 D6
Port of Spain 33 E4
Porto-Novo 73 G5
Porto Velho 36 C3
Port Pirie 80 C4
Port Said 71 F1
Portsmouth (NH) 23 H2
Portsmouth (OH) 27 E3
Portsmouth (U.K.) 45 F5
Portsmouth (VA) 23 F5
Port Sudan 71 F3
Port Talbot 45 E5
Portugal 46 A3
Posadas 37 D5
Potchefstroom 76 B3
Potenza 52 C3
Potomac R. 23 E4
Potosi 36 C4
Potsdam 50 C1
Poughkeepsie 23 G3
Powder R. 29 F1
Powell L. 29 E3
Poznań 50 D1
Prague 50 D2
Praia 72 B2
Prato 52 B2
Prescott 29 E4
Presidente Prudente 37 D5

Presque Isle 23 I1
Preston 45 E4
Pretoria 76 B3
Pribram 50 D2
Prijedor 52 C2
Prince Albert 18 B3
Prince Edward I. 19 D3
Prince Edward Is. 85
Prince George 18 A3
Prince of Wales I. 19 C2
Prince Patrick I. 86
Prince Rupert 18 A3
Pristina 53 D2
Providence 23 H3
Providenciya 55 I1
Provo 29 E2
Prut R. 53 F1
Przemysl 51 F2
Pucallpa 36 B3
Puebla 30 E4
Pueblo 29 G3
Puerto de Santa Maria 46 B4
Puertollano 46 C3
Puerto Montt 37 B7
Puerto Plata 33 C3
Puerto Rico 33 D3
Puerto Rico Trench 84
Pula 52 B2
Puławy 51 F2
Puncak Jaya 67 E4
Pune 63 C5
Punta Arenas 37 B8
Purus R. 36 C3
Pusan 65 F2
Putumayo R. 36 B3
Pyongyang 65 E2
Pyrenees 42 D5

Q

Qatar 60 D3
Qattara Depression 71 E2
Qazvin 60 D1
Qena 71 F2
Qilian Mts. 64 C2
Qingdao 65 E2
Qinghai L. 64 C2
Qiqihar 65 E1
Qom 60 D2
Qonduz 62 B1
Quebec 19 D3
Queen Charlotte Is. 18 A3
Queensland 80 D3
Queenstown 76 B3
Quelimane 76 C2
Querétaro 30 D3
Quetta 62 B2
Quezaltenango 31 F5
Quincy 27 C2
Qui Nhon 66 B2
Quito 36 B3

R

Rabat 70 B1
Rabaul 80 E1
Rach Gia 66 B2
Racine 27 D2
Radom 51 E2
Ragged I. 32 C2
Ragusa 52 C4
Rainier, Mt. 28 C1
Rainy L. 26 C1
Raipur 63 E4
Rajahmundry 63 E5
Rajkot 62 C4
Rajshahi 63 F4
Raleigh 25 G1
Ramat Gan 59 C3
Rancagua 37 B6
Ranchi 63 F4
Randers 48 E5
Rapid City 26 A2

Rasht 60 C1
Rauma 48 H4
Ravenna 52 B2
Ravensburg 50 B3
Rawalpindi 63 C2
Rawlins 29 F2
Razgrad 53 F2
Reading (PA) 23 F3
Reading (U.K.) 45 F5
Recife 36 F3
Red Deer 18 B3
Red Lakes 26 C1
Red R. (USA) 24 D2
Red R. (Vietnam) 66 B1
Red Sea 71 F4
Red Volta R. 73 F4
Regensburg 50 C2
Reggio di Calabria 52 C3
Reggio nell'Emilia 52 B2
Regina 18 B3
Ré, Ile de 42 C3
Reims 43 F2
Rennes 42 C2
Reno 28 D3
Republican R. 26 B2
Resistencia 37 D5
Resita 53 D2
Réunion 85
Reus 47 F2
Revilla Gigedo Is. 83
Reykjavik 48 A2
Reynosa 30 E2
Rhine R. 50 B2
Rhode Island 23 H3
Rhodes 53 F3
Rhodope Mts. 53 E3
Rhone R. 43 F4
Rhum 45 C2
Ribeirão Préto 37 E5
Richmond (Australia) 80 D3
Richmond (VA) 23 F4
Rift Valley 75 C2
Riga 54 A2
Rigestan Desert 62 A2
Rijeka 52 C2
Rimini 52 B2
Ringerike 48 E4
Riobamba 36 B3
Rio Bravo del Norte,see Rio Grande
Rio Cuarto 37 C6
Rio de Janeiro 37 E5
Rio Grande 24 A2, 30 D2
Rivera 37 D6
Riyadh 60 C4
Rize 59 E1
Road Town 33 E3
Roanne 43 F3
Roanoke 22 E5
Robson, Mt. 18 B3
Rochester (MN) 26 C2
Rochester (NH) 23 H2
Rochester (NY) 23 E2
Rockford 27 D2
Rockhampton 80 E3
Rock Hill 25 F2
Rock I. 27 C2
Rock R. 27 D2
Rock Springs 29 F2
Rocky Mount 25 G1
Rocky Mts. 18 A3, 29 E2
Rodez 42 E4
Rodrigues Is. 85
Roeselare 42 E1
Rogers, Mt. 22 D5
Rolla 27 C3
Romania 53 E2
Rome (GA) 25 E2
Rome (Italy) 52 B3
Rosa, Mt. 52 A2
Rosario 37 C6
Roscommon 44 B4

Roscrea 44 C4
Roseau 33 E3
Rosslare 45 C4
Ross Sea 87
Rostock 50 C1
Rostov 54 A2
Rotherham 45 F4
Rotterdam 50 A2
Rouen 42 D2
Rovaniemi 49 I2
Ruapehu, Mt. 81 G4
Rub al Khali 60 C5
Rugby 26 B1
Rukwa L. 75 C2
Rum Cay 32 C2
Rundu 76 A2
Ruse 53 E2
Russian Federation 54 B2
Ruston 24 D2
Rutland 23 G2
Ruvuma R. 76 C1
Ruwenzori Range 75 C1
Rwanda 75 C2
Ryazan 54 A2
Ryukyu Is. 65 E3
Rzeszów 51 F2

S

Saarbrücken 50 B2
Sabadell 47 G2
Sabah 67 C3
Sable, Cape 19 D3
Sacramento 28 C3
Sacramento R. 28 C3
Safi 70 B1
Sagar 63 D4
Saginaw 27 E2
Sagunto 47 E3
Sahara 70 C2
Saharanpur 63 D3
Sahel 70 C3
Saidpur 63 F3
Saint John 19 D3
St. Albans 45 F5
St. Andrews 45 E2
St. Austell 45 D5
St-Brieuc 42 B2
St. Christopher-Nevis 33 E3
St. Cloud 26 C1
St. Croix R. 26 C1
St-Denis 42 E2
St-Dié 43 G2
St-Dizier 43 F2
St-Etienne 43 F4
St. Gallen 43 H3
St. George's 33 E4
St. George's Channel 45 D4
St. Helena 84
St. Helens, Mt. 28 C1
St. Helier 45 H5
St. John's (Antigua) 33 E3
St. John's (Canada) 19 E3
St. Joseph 26 C3
St. Kilda 44 B2
St. Lawrence R. 19 D3
St. Louis (MO) 27 C3
St. Louis (Senegal) 72 C3
St. Lucia 33 E4
St-Malo 42 C2
St. Marc 33 C3
St. Martin 33 E3
St. Moritz 43 H3
St-Nazaire 42 B3
St. Paul 26 C2
St. Paul I. 85
St. Peter & St. Paul Rocks 84
St. Peter Port 45 H5
St. Petersburg (FL) 25 F3
St. Petersburg (Russia) 54 A2
St. Pierre & Miquelon 19 E3

94